喚醒你的英文語感 ！

Get a Feel for English !

喚醒你的英文語感！

Get a Feel for English !

"Foreword" for "Action!"

Cut the crap and let's get going! It's time to learn how to talk about "action!" You're going to have to read this book aloud, and do it a lot, but don't worry! This book is a lot of fun to read and it includes a CD to show you how. Trust me. I know because I recorded the CD with six friends of mine from UC Berkeley (Abby, Anelise, Kelly Anne, Michael, Patricia, and Justin) and we all had a great time playing all the colorful characters in this book. Whether you're sliding down a burning ladder with both pistols blazing or massaging the boulders out of someone's shoulders with hot oil, just learn to mimic the CD and you'll be "talking like a star" in no time!

Brian Greene

少說廢話，動起來吧！讓我們開始學「動作」怎麼說！你必須大聲朗讀本書、勤加練習，但別擔心！這本書讀起來很有趣，而且還附了一片CD教你怎麼開口說。相信我！因為我錄了這張 CD，所以我知道。跟我一起進錄音室的還有加州大學柏克萊分校的六位朋友（Abby、Anelise、Kelly Anne、Michael、Patricia 和 Justin），扮演這本書裡面鮮活的角色，我們都覺得很開心。無論你是一邊溜下著火的梯子，一邊雙手開槍，或是用熱油幫人按摩消除肩膀硬塊，只要學著模仿 CD 的示範，立刻就能在言談間展露「明星風采」！

序——聽自己說英文

　　據聯合國的統計，世界上超過四千種語言中，只有不到八十種有書寫文字。可見語言在溝通上最常使用、也最實用的表達方式是口說。英文與中文一樣源遠流長，無論口說與書寫均已累積相當多年的歷史和使用習慣，學習起來有規可循，但相對地也更要求正確表達，所以能說與能寫是學習英語的人的兩大高難度挑戰。

　　寫作的訓練需要長時間而有紀律地培養，就算母語人士也不一定能駕馭（你遇到過幾過中文表達典雅而很有深度的本國人？）但是說話常常是基於生存需要，能滿足適時表達的需求，因而相較於聽、讀、和寫，使用頻率最高，所以要學會基本的應對並不困難。但要說得頂呱呱或有氣質，除了發音技巧外，更要經常開口練習。國人沒有機會常跟外國人對話，不過也不必因此而放棄練習口說，下面教你一個很有效的提昇英文能力的方法。

打開嗓門，大聲朗讀

　　多數人都同意溝通最常見的方法是對話，學外語如果光是注意語法和單字，結果只能讀而不能說，無法直接交談，就不能達到最有效的溝通目的。從台灣傳統的外語學習流程來看，口說是比較後面的階段。很多受過 ESL 或 EFL 訓練的專家學者曾經質疑過這個流程，認為應該先或同時培養同學開口說的習慣，養成對語言的感覺，慢慢下來自然會說得流利，學會正確表達。無論你同意哪一種方法，大聲朗讀都是學習外語過程中絕對不能少的訓練項目。尤其在初階學習階段，養成朗讀的習慣長久下來對培養語感及使用外語的自然正確功不可沒。

朗讀學英文的效果今日已經普遍被肯定，道理其實很簡單。聲音跟光或其他外在刺激一樣，是一種刺激源，會使大腦產生一定的反應。若是把聲音有規律地重覆用在學習用途上，就等於是一種慢性導入裝置。一定時間之後會變成一種熟悉而慣用的接收（學習）模式，所接收的內容也愈來愈不覺得陌生。但因為每個人的學習背景和對外語的抗拒度不同，要到達自然吸收的境界可能要花上長短不一的時間，一般來說六個月少不了。一旦到達自然吸收的階段，便會對外語產生一種似曾相識的感覺，好像對這個語言已經不再陌生了。這時候你會發現在閱讀一篇外文文章的前面部份時，隱約覺得文章的後面似乎會出現某些句法或語氣；或是你在讀一句句子的前端，會忽然覺得後面已經知道了。這就是所謂「語感」，也就是類似母語的本能（但仍舊很初步）。這時候你會習慣地期待某個動詞後面會出現固定的介詞，某個動詞通常會和某一副詞連用等，而且開始對期待之外、無端出現的語法感到陌生懷疑而需要進一步查個清楚。這個時候的你，其實跟外語已經發生了「超友誼」關係；你和外語之間出現了一段蜜月期。這個蜜月期可能維持不久，不過這是另一個話題。

要藉由朗讀到達這種境界，可以嘗試下面的簡單方法：先挑一段100字左右的短文或對話，仔細解讀一兩遍；將所有不懂的生字及慣用語都標示出再查字典，然後尋找一個不會干擾別人的地方，將這段短文大聲朗讀 10 到

15 遍，之後休息一下，再拿起筆來寫一段長度相當的段落。寫的時候切記將原來那段文章中你很欣賞的生字或慣用語應用到你自己的段落中。只要你有恆心，至少六個月內每天晚上睡前都這樣做，保證你能培養出初步的語感。但有一個先決條件：你對發音必須有一定程度的掌握，而且選擇用來朗讀的原文要適合你的程度，不能太艱深。這兩項困難都得靠適合的輔助學習工具來克服。其實拿捏發音的規則及朗讀的正面效果有賴於取材的正確。

貝塔語言出版的《朗讀學英文》系列內容深淺適中，對大多數人來說都適合。系列作者都是曾受高等教育的母語人士、隨書附贈的 CD 也皆是由錄音經驗豐富的專業人士所錄製，對讀者掌握及反覆練習正確的發音很有幫助。再次提醒諸位，藉由大聲朗讀而提升對英語的感覺和加強口說能力需要一段時間和耐力。今日在台灣，學外語是一種報酬率相當高的投資。無論你做的是哪一行，每天花個十五分鐘提升一輩子的口說能力，擴大自己的就業機會，使自己更有價值，何樂不為？

大聲朗讀還有兩個令人滿意的效果：一是舌頭很快會變得更靈活，轉動敏捷流暢，較不會「卡帶」。二是原來很不熟悉或不存在於中文的聲音，持續練習後會領悟到發音的竅門。

Read on!

梁欣榮 2005.8.4
國立台灣大學外國語文學系副教授

行行止止、或高或低：抑揚頓挫的藝術

從小聽英文老師說「你好嗎？」（"How are you?"）要使勁念作「好阿儒」，「阿」的旁邊還常劃上一道往上陡升的曲線或箭頭，到了「儒」立刻急速下降。長大後在實際英語操作情境中有時卻聽到人淡淡的說 "How are you?"，句中的高音不但遠不如之前的「阿」，而且似乎還落在結尾的 you 字上。尤其是像 "How are you today?" 或 "How are you, sir?" 等句子。

除非像附帶問句（tag questions）這類少數特殊結構，習慣利用音調的升降來暗示說話的人的立場（句末音調上揚表示真正的疑問，下降則表示發問人對前面直述句充滿自信，（如：You like fish, don't you?），無論是中文或英文，說話音調的上揚或下降雖受制於語言習慣，但嚴格說來少有絕對的規則。

毫無疑問，音調是意義的一部份，所以在缺乏實際溝通狀況下常常無法斷言某一句子一定得上揚或下降。影響句子音調的高低除了語言文字的歷史因素之外，還有具體的情境及文化因素。譬如說話的人可能累了，聽的人可能患重聽，你可能正在火冒三丈，他也許正在遲疑或膽怯等等。這些因素都會直接影響句子音調的高低。此外，還有地域、鄉音、族群、年齡等因素，也都足以影響說話音調的高低（聽過可愛的馬來西亞僑生或山東同胞說國語的人應該會同意我這個說法）。

除了高低音之外，說話或朗讀時還有停頓和加速的考量。停頓跟高低音一樣，常受到語言習慣或演化的規範，也受文化及地域影響（聽說廣東人說話都像開機關槍一樣，響個不停），落點同樣不一定絕對。停頓的原因有很多，下面是較明顯的例子：

1. **意義單元的停頓**：如標點符號前後，句子的開始或結束等。
2. **自然音調的停頓**：如轉接詞或感歎詞之後（Ah, well, anyway...）。
3. **句子結構的停頓**：如前置 If 子句與後面主要子句間的停頓，或列舉表達方式（A, B, or C.）的停頓。
4. **策略運用的停頓**：如製造懸疑或期待，加強語氣等。
5. **人的因素的停頓**：如說話的人疲倦、表達疑慮、需要換氣、情緒起伏等。
6. **修辭藝術的停頓**：如十四世紀英國首韻詩每一行中間都有一停頓（學名為 caesura，例 "In summer season // when soft was the sun"）

　　停頓和音調高低都隱約有規可循，但也都無法可管。《朗讀學英文》系列基本上不標示音調的高低，僅標示可停頓及語氣加重之處。所以讀本書時最重要的是先融入章節中的情境。先了解每一段獨白的發生場景、主題、說話的人的大概年齡和心境。掌握這些要素後，再反覆細心聆聽附贈光碟的錄音，才能充分感受到音調變化及明白標示的停頓與強調處的自然合理。同時你也會了解到，這些標示只是輔助，而不是絕對唯一。一旦時空背景等因素改變，同一段獨白輕重音的落點很可能會有不同，而停頓的次數也會因人而異。可能的話，不妨請幾位外國朋友試讀同一段，保證會有意想不到的效果。

梁欣榮 2005.8.23
國立台灣大學外國語文學系副教授

學習設計

　　本書著重「口語表達能力」的訓練，因此在設計上強調聽和說的練習。本書每一章節穿插著聽、說、讀等不同的學習活動，期能幫助讀者循序漸進地培養口語表達能力。不過，由於每個人感興趣的範圍不同，所以讀者在使用時，或許就會照自己的需求來決定閱讀的順序，而不會按照本書固有的設計；但我們還是建議讀者，可以採取本書所規劃的學習步驟及每日十五分鐘的時間安排，並從中獲益。以下便將一章當中，學習步驟的設計理念說明如下：

學習設計：

目　標	步驟搭配
瞭解文意 本書每段朗讀文章在 100 字左右，仔細解讀 1~2 遍，熟悉生字及慣用語。	先聽故事： 一段以「倒述」或「重回現場」的手法實況演出內容，用耳朵感受歷歷在目的畫面。
⬇ 朗讀訓練 掌握正確發音、語調、聲音表情。每天大聲跟讀一篇文章 10 到 15 遍。	1. 分解動作：理解基本用語，扎實敘述功力。 2. 發音秘笈：破除發音錯誤或咬字含糊。 3. 口才練功房：重播故事橋段，自然而然學會流利描述連續動作。 4. 心法修練：自我測驗文章內容。 5. 變化招式：領悟動作其他含義，如 kick 是「踢」，for kicks 是「找刺激」。
⬇ 喚醒語感 讓聲音隨時間成為一種慢性導入裝置，達到自然吸收的效果。當舌頭變得靈動敏捷，熟悉原不存在於中文的英語發音。這時就大功告成了。	○ 發音秘笈 ○ 口才練功房 ○ 心法修練 重複做6 個月

Contents

Interview Clips
專訪特輯

Contents

Delinquent Youth

輕狂少年時期

比利，大家都知道你是個馳名的電影明星。你不怕死的特技演出和不可思議的動作場面已經讓你的電影在世界各地大受歡迎造成轟動。許多影迷都知道你是在灣仔長大的，當時的灣仔是個龍蛇混雜的地方──如果想找麻煩，到那兒就對了。從我聽到的一些故事，似乎你自己也製造過不少麻煩。但是有些故事聽起來和你某部電影中的情節似乎有雷同之處，不禁啓人疑竇。到底哪些是真的，哪些是虛構的？實在很難判斷。你真的曾經在香港四處閒蕩找人幹架嗎？那時的你真是街頭上最剽悍的小子嗎？你真的蹲過苦窯嗎？告訴我們實情吧，比利。

Billy, everybody knows that you are a famous movie star. Your daredevil stunts and incredible action scenes have made your films hits all over the world. A lot of your fans also know that you grew up in Wanchai, which was at that time a rough-and-tumble neighborhood—a good place to go if you were looking for trouble. Based on some of the stories I've heard, it seems like you caused a fair bit of trouble yourself. But sometimes the stories sound suspiciously like scenes from one of your movies. Which are fact and which fiction? It's hard to tell. Did you really go roaming about Hong Kong, picking fights? Were you really the toughest kid on the street? Did you really spend time in jail? Tell us the truth, Billy.

[01]

ALLEY CAT
小混混
Street Fighting 街頭打鬥

說灣仔是三教九流之地，一點也沒錯。我確實三天二頭就找人幹架，在那種地方要找架打也不難。要是真的找不到，我就自己製造一場。不知道為什麼，我就是愛打架，到現在也還是。小的時候我個頭不大，甚至有一點矮胖，沒有人料到我幹起架來會是那樣。我令他們大感意外，所以大家都記得我。就這樣，我以惡狠難纏闖出了名號。後來就變得很難找到人幹架了。

Wanchai was rowdy, it's true. I did go looking for a fight pretty often and it wasn't hard to find one. If I couldn't find one, I'd just start one. I don't know why, I just liked to fight. I still do. I was a small kid and a little bit pudgy. Nobody expected me to fight like I did. I surprised them, so they remembered me. That's how I got a reputation for being mean and tough. Then it got harder to find a fight.

CD-02

現場邀請到的是：[古奇曼，比利的兒時玩伴]

Billy Ho was a mean little alley[1] cat. He was always picking fights, just to prove himself. He'd <u>walk right up to</u> the biggest, toughest guy on the street and <u>kick him in the shin</u>, or <u>punch him in the nose</u>. None of this movie star kung-fu. No — he'd <u>poke you in the eye</u>. And he'd <u>pinch and scratch and bite</u>, too. He didn't lose many fights. Even when he did, let me tell you, the winner usually wasn't too eager to repeat[2] the experience.

翻 譯

比利‧何以前是個惡狠狠的小混混，老是在挑釁幹架，就是想證明自己很行。他會直接走到街頭上最壯最兇狠的傢伙面前，在對方的小腿上踢一腳，或在人家的鼻子上揍一拳。用的可不是他現在電影裡的功夫招式。不——他會戳你的眼珠子，甚至又招又抓，外加張嘴咬人。他很少吃敗仗，就算吃了敗仗，我告訴你，贏他的人通常也不會想跟他再幹一架。

Word list | 1. alley [`ælɪ] *n.* 巷子
| 2. repeat [rɪ`pit] *v.* 重複

CD-03

第一步

動作分解：跟唸 3-5 次紮實基本功

o to walk up to somebody	走到某人面前
o to kick somebody in the shin	踢某人的小腿
o to poke somebody in the eye	戳某人的眼睛
o to punch somebody in the nose	揍某人的鼻子
o to pinch, scratch, and bite	又捏、又抓、又咬

第二步

 CD-04

發音秘笈：跟唸 2-3 次，破除你咬字含糊、發音錯誤的弱點

自然發音："o+e" 長音 [o] 與 [u]

大部分字尾拼法是 **"o+e"** 的字，如 nose、poke、hope、coke、globe 等等，"o" 都發長音 [o]，但是有些同樣拼法的字，如 prove、lose、move 等，"o" 都發長音 [u]；換言之，在英語裡拼字相同，發音卻不見得相同。

[練習]

[o]: nose、poke、hope、coke、globe

[u]: prove、lose、move

Why did I **lose** the fight? He **poked** me in the eye and I fell into the pool. But it doesn't **prove** anything. 我為什麼會輸掉這場打鬥？他戳我的眼珠子，然後我又掉進游泳池裡。但這又不能證明什麼。

第三步

CD-02

口才練功房：重新過招，學學「古其曼」的口氣、語調

Billy Ho was a mean little alley cat. He was always picking fights, just to prove himself. He'd walk right up to the biggest, toughest guy on the street / and kick him in the shin, or punch him in the nose. None of this movie star kung-fu. No — he'd poke you in the eye. And he'd pinch / and scratch / and bite, too. He didn't lose many fights. Even when he did, let me tell you, the winner usually wasn't too eager to repeat the experience.

換你朗讀。特別注意：
1. 基本原則請參考 [序2]
2. 如果需要多聽幾次示範，請到 CD-02 [00:23]
3. 請注意停頓、語氣的表現：
　[/]：除了一般英文標點符號以外，可以停頓的地方。
　[套色字]：加重語氣的字。

如果需要再聽幾次，請重播 CD-02 [00:23]

第四步

心法修練：重播 CD，測驗自己習得幾成功力

Billy Ho was a mean little alley cat. He was always picking fights, just to prove himself. He'd _____ the biggest, toughest guy on the street and _____, or _____. None of this movie star kung-fu. No — he'd _____. And he'd _____, too. He didn't lose many fights. Even when he did, let me tell you, the winner usually wasn't too eager to repeat the experience.

第五步

變化招式：領悟基本動作的另一層意義

for kicks 為尋求刺激、快感（而做某事）

The boys race motorcycles for kicks. 男孩們飆機車，尋求快感。

get a kick out of ... 享受做某事的刺激和快感

I get a kick out of windsurfing. 我喜歡衝浪，很刺激。

a kick in the ass 教訓一頓

James is intelligent, but a little lazy — he just needs a kick in the ass, and he'll do fine. 詹姆士很聰明，就是有一點懶——只要給他一頓教訓，就沒問題了。

【02】

HATCHET HANDS
快斧手

Vandalism 搞破壞

我以前是個毛躁的小孩，在學校坐著上一整天的課對我來說簡直是種苦刑。通常我都熬不下去。我知道十多條不同的「逃亡」路線。我會偷溜出去，在附近閒晃一整天。校外有很多有趣的人可以聊天，還有很多好玩的東西可以看。偶爾我也會打些零工，譬如在水果攤堆芒果，或者幫某個店家清掃門口。有的時候，如果找不到事做，我就闖禍。

chapter 02 ▶

I was a restless kid. Sitting through a full day of school was torture for me. Usually I didn't make it. I had a dozen different escape routes. I'd slip out and spend the day wandering around the neighborhood. There were lots of interesting people to talk to and lots of things to see. Occasionally I picked up an odd job, stacking mangoes at a fruit stall or sweeping somebody's storefront. Sometimes, when I couldn't find anything else to do, I got into trouble.

現場邀請到的是：[哈洛・王，影評兼傳記作家]

How did Billy Ho get his nickname[1]? He went about his neighborhood <u>chopping things into pieces</u>. He <u>hacked</u> through plank fences. He <u>shattered</u> plastic signs. He tried to <u>bend</u> water pipes. He chopped mirrors from cars and motor scooters. He'd <u>climb</u> <u>three stories</u> <u>up to</u> somebody's balcony[2] just to <u>snap</u> <u>a bamboo clothes pole</u> <u>in half</u>. They started calling him Hatchet[3] Hands. Eventually, to teach him a lesson, the police <u>threw him into</u> <u>the local jail</u>. He chopped through a brick wall and walked out.

翻譯

　　比利・何的綽號是怎麼來的？他在住家附近搞破壞，把東西砍得支離破碎。他會劈開柵欄，打碎塑膠招牌。他會企圖扳彎水管，剁掉汽機車上的鏡子。他還會爬上三樓到人家的陽臺上，只是為了把曬衣服的竹竿折成兩半。於是大家開始管他叫快斧手。到最後，警察把他送進當地的監牢裡，想給他一點教訓，但他卻劈開磚牆，一走了之。

Word list | 1. nickname [ˋnɪk.nem] *n.* 綽號　　3. hatchet [ˋhætʃɪt] *n.* 小斧頭
　　　　　　| 2. balcony [ˋbælkənɪ] *n.* 陽台

第一步

動作分解：跟唸 3-5 次紮實基本功

o to chop things into pieces	把東西砍得支離破碎
o to hack	劈、砍
o to shatter	使成碎片
o to bend	使彎曲；扳
o to climb up to [somewhere]	攀爬上（某處）
o to snap [something] in half	折斷（某物）使其變成二半
o to throw somebody into jail	把某人送進監獄

第二步

發音秘笈：跟唸 2-3 次，破除你咬字含糊、發音錯誤的弱點

停頓／聲調

★ How did Billy get his nickname? / He went about ...

影評兼傳記作家哈洛‧王先生先在提出問句 How did Billy get his nickname? 時，準備自問自答，所以把聲調稍微提高一些。之後則停頓了一會兒，目的是想確定大家有專心在聽他說話。這時，聽者就會知道，接下來的話很重要。

[練習]

1. Have you ever heard the story about Billy and the elephant? / I'll tell you.
   你有沒有聽過比利和大象的故事？／我講給你聽。

2. Did Billy really deserve his reputation as a troublemaker? / You better believe it. 比利真的是個名副其實的頭痛人物嗎？／這你無需懷疑。

第三步

CD-05

口才練功房：重新過招，學學「哈洛·王」的口氣、語調

How did Billy Ho get his nickname? He went about his neighborhood / chopping things into pieces. He hacked through plank fences. He shattered plastic signs. He tried to bend water pipes. He chopped mirrors from cars and motor scooters. He'd climb three stories / up to somebody's balcony / just to snap a bamboo clothes pole in half. They started calling him Hatchet Hands. Eventually, to teach him a lesson, the police threw him into the local jail. He chopped through a brick wall / and walked out.

換你朗讀。特別注意：
1. 基本原則請參考 [序2]
2. 如果需要多聽幾次示範，請到 CD-05 [00:05]
3. 請注意停頓、語氣的表現：
  [/]：除了一般英文標點符號以外，可以停頓的地方。
  [套色字]：加重語氣的字。

如果需要再聽幾次，請重播 CD-05 [00:05]

第四步

心法修練：重播 CD，測驗自己習得幾成功力

How did Billy Ho get his nickname? He went about his neighborhood _____. He _____ through plank fences. He _____ plastic signs. He tried to _____ water pipes. He chopped mirrors from cars and motor scooters. He'd _____ three stories _____ somebody's balcony just to _____ a bamboo clothes pole _____. They started calling him Hatchet Hands. Eventually, to teach him a lesson, the police _____ the local _____. He chopped through a brick wall and walked out.

第五步

變化招式：領悟基本動作的另一層意義

bend somebody's ear 與人說話沒完沒了

I asked my music teacher what the final exam was going to be like, and he bent my ear for an hour about Bach's use of counterpoint. 我問音樂老師期末考要怎麼考，結果他沒完沒了地講了一個小時，述說巴哈如何如何使用對位法。

bent out of shape 很不高興

After you asked for a raise in front of everyone, the boss was really bent out of shape. Next time go to his office. 在你當著大家的面向老闆要求加薪之後，他很不高興。下次到他辦公室去談。

bent on something/doing something 矢志；下決心

Sally is not just bent on winning; she's bent on world domination. 莎莉不僅矢要贏，她矢志要當世界第一。

[03]

JAILBREAK
越獄記

Escape 脫身

　　到現在我都還會回老家去。那裡變了很多。我小時候住的那一棟樓已經拆掉，現在是一家夜總會。不過很多人還是住在原來的地方。我喜歡去那邊買東西，和街上的人聊天，就跟小時候一樣。他們大多已經原諒我以前惹的麻煩，但是並沒有忘記。我有一個朋友是退休員警，到現在他還會談到我越獄的事情。

　　I still go back to the old neighborhood. It's changed a lot. The building where I grew up is gone. There's a nightclub there now. But plenty of people still live where they always did. I like to shop there and chat with people on the street, just as I did when I was a kid. Mostly they've forgiven me for the trouble I caused. But they haven't forgotten. One friend of mine is a retired police officer. He's still talking about my jailbreak.

來看VCR：[潘華德，警察、監獄警衛（第 31 號警察局），
香港灣仔，1959年]

What's that noise? Wai-Man, I'm going back to check on our little street rat. ... Hey! Kid! Stop that! Hey! Wai-Man! Bring the key!? He's escaping[1]! Hurry, Wai-Man — the key! He's <u>knocked a hole in</u> the wall! He's <u>squirming[2] through</u> it right now! <u>Toss</u> me the key! OK, come on, come on ... <u>GET</u> HIM! <u>GRAB</u> HIM! DON'T <u>LET GO</u>! <u>HOLD</u> HIM! Damn. Wai-Man, you got nothing but his shoe. He <u>slipped away</u>. Damn that little vandal[3]. Wai-Man, we're in big trouble now.

翻譯

那是什麼聲音？懷民，我要回去查看一下那個小混混……嘿！小子！住手！嘿！懷民！拿鑰匙來！？他要逃走了！快一點，懷民——鑰匙！他在牆壁上打出了一個洞！他現在正在鑽出去！鑰匙丟給我！好，快點、快點……逮住他！抓住他！不要放手！抓緊他！可惡。懷民，你只抓到他的鞋子。他溜走了。可惡的小破壞狂。懷民，我們現在麻煩大了。

Word list | 1. escape [əˋskep] *v.* 逃脫   3. vandal [ˋvænd!] *n.* 破壞者、摧殘者
         | 2. squirm [skwɝm] *v.* 扭動身體

第一步

動作分解：跟唸 3-5 次紮實基本功

o to knock a hole in something	把某物打出一個洞
o to squirm through [a hole]	扭著身體（鑽出洞）
o to toss [someone] [something]	抛（某物）（給某人）
o to get [somebody]	逮住（某人）
o to grab [somebody]	抓住（某人）
o to let go	放手
o to hold [somebody]	抓緊（某人）
o to slip away	溜走

第二步

發音秘笈：跟唸 2-3 次，破除你咬字含糊、發音錯誤的弱點

連音：come on >> common [ˋkʌˋmɑn]

★ OK, come on, come on …

請再聽一次潘警員的句子，留意片語 "come on" 中的連音。這個片語很常見，非常好用。美國人的唸法為 [ˋkʌˋmɑn]，把 come 的子音 [m] 和 on 的母音 [ɑ] 連在一起唸。

[練習]

1. **Come on**, let's go! 快一點，咱們走吧！

2. What are you waiting for? **Come on**! 你還在磨蹭什麼？快一點！

第三步

CD-08

口才練功房：重新過招，學學「潘華德」的口氣、語調

What's that noise? Wai-Man, I'm going back to check on our little street rat. ... Hey! Kid! Stop that! Hey! Wai-Man! Bring the key!? He's escaping! Hurry, Wai-Man — the key! He's knocked a hole in the wall! He's squirming through it right now! Toss me the key! OK, come on, come on ... GET HIM! GRAB HIM! DON'T LET GO! HOLD HIM! Damn. Wai-Man, you got nothing but his shoe. He slipped away. Damn that little vandal. Wai-Man, we're in big trouble now.

換你朗讀。特別注意：
1. 基本原則請參考 [序2]
2. 如果需要多聽幾次示範，請到 CD-08 [00:05]
3. 請注意停頓、語氣的表現：
　　[/]：除了一般英文標點符號以外，可以停頓的地方。
　　[套色字]：加重語氣的字。

第四步

心法修練：重播CD，測驗自己習得幾成功力

What's that noise? Wai-Man, I'm going back to check on our little street rat. ... Hey! Kid! Stop that! Hey! Wai-Man! Bring the key!? He's escaping! Hurry, Wai-Man — the key! He's _____ the wall! He's _____ it right now! _____ me the key! OK, come on, come on ... _____ HIM! _____ HIM! DON'T_____! _____ HIM! Damn. Wai-Man, you got nothing but his shoe. He _____ _____ . Damn that little vandal. Wai-Man, we're in big trouble now.

第五步

變化招式：領悟基本動作的另一層意義

grab someone's attention 吸引某人注意

A good newspaper headline should grab everyone's attention. 好的報紙頭條應該要能吸引每個人的注意。

How does that grab you? 你覺得怎麼樣？

If you work for me, I'll pay you $1,000,000 per year. How does that grab you? 如果你幫我工作，我就付你年薪一百萬。你覺得怎麼樣？

up for grabs 人人有機會獲得某物

Nobody ate the chocolate ice cream. If it's up for grabs, I'll eat it. 那巧克力冰淇淋沒人吃。如果誰都可以吃的話，那我就不客氣了。

【04】

MA HO
何媽媽

Home 在家的時候

以前翹課的話，我媽就會罰我跪在地上二小時，一面看書。我的乖戾行徑讓我媽痛苦——也讓我自己痛苦。哈、哈！後來我不得不退學去工作，讓她的心都碎了。我跑到巴西，音訊全無的時候，她還以為我死了。最近我已經安份了些。我人在香港的時候幾乎每天都會去看她，一起笑談過去的事情。

For skipping school, my mom used to make me kneel on the floor for three hours, reading a book. My misbehavior was hard on her — and hard on me, too. Ha, ha! When I had to leave school to work, it broke her heart. When I disappeared to Brazil, she thought I was dead. These days, I've settled down a bit. I see her almost every day when I'm in Hong Kong, and we always laugh about those old times.

現場邀請到的是：[何媽媽，比利的母親]

Hatchet Hands? That was his *street* name. At *home*, we had another name for Billy. Little Earthquake[1]. He was always <u>tearing about</u>. He couldn't <u>sit still</u>. His favorite game was to <u>line up</u> some chairs and then try to <u>leap from one to the next</u>. He kept moving them further and further apart until he missed and <u>fell and crashed onto the floor</u>. Mr. Tam from downstairs would get mad and <u>bang on</u> his ceiling[2] with a broom handle. Said it was like living underneath a non-stop earthquake.

翻譯

　　快斧手？那是他的街頭稱號。在家裡，我們都叫他另外一個名字——小地震。比利片刻不得閒，總是坐不住。他最喜歡玩的遊戲就是把幾張椅子排成一排，然後從這一張跳到下一張。他不斷搬動椅子，把它們排得一次比一次遠，非到最後跳不過去，摔在地上才肯罷休。樓下的譚先生常常氣得用掃帚的手把敲天花板，說他就像住在永無休止的地震下方。

Word list
1. earthquake [ˋɝθˏkwek] *n.* 地震
2. ceiling [ˋsilɪŋ] *n.* 天花板

CD-12

第一步

動作分解：跟唸 **3-5** 次紮實基本功

o to tear about	到處亂闖；胡搞瞎搞
o to sit still	坐得住
o to line up something	把某物排成一排
o to leap from one to the next	從一個跳到下一個
o to fall and crash onto the floor	跌落撞到地板上
o to bang [on something]	猛烈敲打（某物）

CD-13

第二步

發音秘笈：跟唸 **2-3** 次，破除你咬字含糊、發音錯誤的弱點

加重語氣：

★ That was his *street* name. At *home* we had another name for Billy.

注意聽比利的媽媽在說 "street" 和 "home" 兩個字時，把說話速度放慢，並提高了聲調，目的是為了凸顯出兩者的差別。

[練習]

1. It's not **what** you say; it's **how** you say it.
   重點不是你說什麼；是你怎麼說。

2. I didn't **want** to do it, but I **had** to do it.
   我不想這麼做，但我必須這麼做。

第三步

口才練功房：重新過招，學學「何媽媽」的口氣、語調　*CD-11*

　　Hatchet Hands? That was his *street* name. At *home*, we had another name for Billy. Little Earthquake. He was always tearing about. He couldn't sit still. His favorite game was to line up some chairs / and then try to leap / from one to the next. He kept moving them further and further apart / until he missed / and fell and crashed onto the floor. Mr. Tam from downstairs would get mad / and bang on his ceiling with a broom handle. Said / it was like living underneath a non-stop earthquake.

換你朗讀。特別注意：

1. 基本原則請參考 [序2]

2. 如果需要多聽幾次示範，請到 CD-11 [00:05]

3. 請注意停頓、語氣的表現：

　　[/]：除了一般英文標點符號以外，可以停頓的地方。

　　[套色字]：加重語氣的字。

如果需要再聽幾次，請重播 **CD-11** [00:05]

第四步

心法修練： 重播 CD，測驗自己習得幾成功力

Hatchet Hands? That was his *street* name. At *home*, we had another name for Billy. Little Earthquake. He was always _____ . He couldn't _____ . His favorite game was to _____ some chairs and then try to _____ _____ . He kept moving them further and further apart until he missed and _____ . Mr. Tam from downstairs would get mad and _____ his ceiling with a broom handle. Said it was like living underneath a non-stop earthquake.

第五步

變化招式： 領悟基本動作的另一層意義

crash 睡覺

I've been working since 8:00 a.m. without a break — I'm going to go home now and crash. 我從早上八點就開始工作，一直沒歇過——現在要回家呼呼大睡了。

a crash course 速成班

Mindy just found out she's being transferred to Germany next month, so she's going to take a crash course in German. 明蒂剛得知下個月公司要把她調到德國去，所以她要去上德文速成班。

crash a party 不在受邀名單卻自己出席宴會

Of course I don't know Julia Roberts — but I heard she had invited two hundred guests to her house, so I just crashed the party. 我當然不認識茱莉亞蘿勃茲——但我聽說她邀請了二百名客人到她家，所以我就不請自來了。

【05】

SCHOOL
學生時代

Leaving Class in a Hurry
衝出教室

我的確喜歡學新東西。在巴西的時候，我學會了讀寫葡萄牙文。信不信由你，最近我在學英文──他們要我把以前拍的電影其中幾部重新配音，翻成英文版。我從一些 CD 上來學；我到山上散步時邊走邊聽。我的問題是，我就是受不了乖乖坐在教室裡。小時候受不了，現在還是受不了。

I do like to learn stuff. I learned to read and write Portuguese while I was in Brazil, and these days, believe it or not, I'm studying English —they want me to dub some of my own old movies into English. I'm learning from some CDs. I listen while I go walking in the hills. The thing with me is that I just can't stand sitting in a classroom. I couldn't stand it when I was a kid, and I can't stand it now.

CD-14

Sit still, Billy! Billy! I mean it. I'll <u>throttle</u>[1] you good. And don't even think about <u>climbing out that window</u> again. I saw that glance, Billy. You won't make it. No way. I'll <u>catch</u> you and I'll <u>beat you black and blue</u>. Oh, you're a handful[2], but I'll train you yet. I will not permit[3] you to disrupt[4] my class. <u>Sit back down</u>, Billy. Don't you dare <u>take another step</u> towards that window. I mean it. Don't do it. Billy! BILLY! <u>Get back here</u>!

翻 譯

　　坐好！比利！比利！我可不是說著玩的。我會活活招死你。你甭想從那扇窗爬上去。我看到你的目光了，比利。你辦不到的。門兒都沒有。我會抓到你，把你揍得青一塊紫一塊。哦，你真叫人頭痛，不過我會好好訓練你，絕不允許你干擾我上課。回位子上坐好，比利。你敢再往那扇窗戶踏出一步試試看。我可不是說著玩的。別這樣做。比利！！比利！！你給我回來！

Word list | 1. throttle [ˋθrɑtl] *v.* 勒住喉嚨　　　　3. permit [pɚˋmɪt] *v.* 允許
　　　　　　2. handful [ˋhænd͵fʊl] *n.* 棘手的人　　4. disrupt [dɪsˋrʌpt] *v.* 打斷

第一步

動作分解：跟唸 3-5 次紮實基本功

o to throttle someone	掐死某人
o to climb out a window	爬出窗戶
o to catch [somebody]	抓住（某人）
o to beat somebody black and blue	把某人打得青一塊紫一塊
o Sit back down!	回去做好！
o to take a step	踏出一步
o Get back here!	給我回來！

第二步

發音秘笈：跟唸 2-3 次，破除你咬字含糊、發音錯誤的弱點

連音："-(t)ch" 或 "-t" 與 "you" 的連音

當 "you" 的前面出現 "-(t)ch" 或 "-t" 時，連起來念就像 [tʃu]，甚至像 [dʒu]。請再聽一次以下幾個句子：

[練習]

1. I'll **catch you** and I'll **beat you** black and blue.

2. I will not **permit you** to disrupt my class.

3. **Don't you** dare.

＊注意，當 "you" 接在其他字母之後，不會出現這種唸法變化：

4. I'll train you yet.

第三步

口才練功房：重新過招，學學「張老師」的口氣、語調

Sit still, Billy! Billy! I mean it. I'll throttle you good. And

don't even think about climbing out that window again. I saw

that glance, Billy. You won't make it. No way. I'll catch you

/and I'll beat you black and blue. Oh, you're a handful, but

I'll train you yet. I will not permit you / to disrupt my class.

Sit back down, Billy. Don't you dare / take another step

towards that window. I mean it. Don't do it. Billy! BILLY! Get

back here!

換你朗讀。特別注意：
1. 基本原則請參考 [序2]
2. 如果需要多聽幾次示範，請到 CD-14 [00:06]
3. 請注意停頓、語氣的表現：
   [/]：除了一般英文標點符號以外，可以停頓的地方。
   [套色字]：加重語氣的字。

第四步

心法修練：重播CD，測驗自己習得幾成功力

Sit still, Billy! Billy! I mean it. I'll _____ you good. And don't even think about _____ again. I saw that glance, Billy. You won't make it. No way. I'll _____ you and I'll _____. Oh, you're a handful, but I'll train you yet. I will not permit you to disrupt my class. _____ , Billy. Don't you dare _____ towards that window. I mean it. Don't do it. Billy! BILLY! _____!

第五步

變化招式：領悟基本動作的另一層意義

step it up 更加倍付出或努力

While preparing for your final exams, you may feel it is necessary to step it up and study harder than usual. 準備期末考的時候，你可能會覺得必須加倍努力，比平常更用功。

step on it 加快速度

You're not finished getting dressed yet? Step on it— we're going to be late! 你衣服還沒穿好？快點——我們要遲到了！

step on someone's toes 冒犯某人；觸怒某人

I think you stepped on Richard's toes by modifying our web site without asking him first. He usually takes care of all our company's web design, you know. 你沒先問理查你就自行修改了我們的網站，我想你把他惹毛了。你可知道我們公司所有的網頁設計通常都由他負責。

Woks and Docks

炒菜鍋和碼頭的時光

　　比利，你很晚才進入電影圈，一直到三十五歲才第一次在電影裡擔任主角。你年輕的時候，做過哪些工作？你真的為澳門黑道賣過命嗎？請告訴我們你在成名之前，是如何餬口的。

　　Billy, you got a late start in the movie business. You didn't have your first starring role in a film until you were thirty-five years old. What kinds of jobs did you do as a young man? Is it true that you worked for the Macau mafia? Tell us how you supported yourself before you made it big.

[06]

DOWN PEEL STREET
混扒皮街的日子
Daredevil Bike Riding
騎鐵馬亂竄

　　我第一份真正的差事是當騎腳踏車送貨的小弟。那時我十二歲，一天到晚蹺課，但我可不是懶惰蟲。我很努力工作，我必須幫忙扶養我的母親和小妹妹。我們有一輛老舊的紅色腳踏車，只有一段速度，雖然對我而言有點大，但是我還是學會了騎它，而且還騎得挺順的。一名叫老劉的生意人看到我騎著腳踏車到處衝，就雇用我幫他跑腿。

　　My first real job was as a bicycle delivery boy. I was twelve. I skipped school a lot, but I wasn't lazy. I worked hard. I had to help support my mother and my kid sister. We had an old red bike. It had just one speed and it was a little big for me, but I learned to ride it and I got pretty good. A businessman named Lau saw me racing around and he hired me to run errands for him.

chapter 06

來看VCR：[方美拉，路邊小販，香港，1961 年]

Did you see that? That kid is on a suicide[1] mission. He <u>races down</u> Peel Street like that every day. <u>Measures the gaps</u> on the fly[2], <u>cuts between</u> cars, <u>hops</u> curbs[3], <u>dodges</u> dogs. Sooner or later, he'll <u>wipe out</u> and <u>break his neck</u>. He never touches the brakes. Not until he makes the bottom and then he always <u>goes into a big skid</u>[4] around the corner and disappears into the traffic on Queen's Road. You watch — he'll be <u>smeared</u>[5] all over Peel Street one of these days.

翻譯

你看到沒有？那小子根本是趕著去投胎。他每天像那樣從扒皮街一路往下衝，衝忙地在汽車間找空隙，東鑽西竄，一下子騎上人行道，一會兒閃避狗兒。他早晚會翻車跌斷頸子。他一路都不踩煞車，總是一直騎到底才在轉角處猛地甩尾，然後消失在皇后路的車陣當中。看著吧——總有一天，他會在扒皮街上摔得遍體鱗傷。

Word list | 1. suicide [ˋsuəˌsaɪd] *n.* 自殺 | 4. skid [skɪd] *n.*（車子）橫滑
| 2. on the fly 忙來忙去地 | 5. smear [smɪr] *v.* 塗抹；【俚】打
| 3. curb [kɝb] *n.*（人行道）路緣

CD-18

第一步

動作分解：跟唸 **3-5** 次紮實基本功

o to race down	往下衝
o to measure the gaps	找空隙
o to cut between ...	插到……之間
o to hop	蹦跳
o to dodge	閃躲
o to wipe out	翻覆
o to break one's neck	摔斷頸子
o to go into a skid	打滑；甩尾
o to smear	塗抹；弄髒；【俚】打敗

第二步

CD-19

發音秘笈：跟唸 **2-3** 次，破除你咬字含糊、發音錯誤的弱點

困難發音：[ʒ] vs. [dʒ]

★ **Measures** the gaps on the fly,... **dodges** dogs.

再聽一次方美蕾的錄音，留意 measure 中的 [ʒ] 音和 dodge 中的 [dʒ] 音。[ʒ] 是一個純粹的磨擦音，切勿與 [dʒ] 這個爆擦音) 混淆。

[練習]

[ʒ]：measure、treasure、pleasure、television、massage、Asia、garage、beige

[dʒ]：dodge、message、geography、general

1. I think studying **geography** is a real **pleasure**.
   我認為研讀地理學真的是一件樂事。

2. In **Asia**, I had to **dodge** a lot of scooters.
   在亞洲時，我得要閃躲很多摩托車。

第三步

口才練功房：重新過招，學學「方美拉」的口氣、語調

Did you see that? That kid is on a suicide mission. He races down Peel Street like that every day. Measures the gaps on the fly, cuts between cars, hops curbs, dodges dogs. Sooner or later, he'll wipe out / and break his neck. He never touches the brakes. Not until he makes the bottom / and then he always goes into a big skid around the corner / and disappears into the traffic on Queen's Road. You watch — he'll be smeared all over Peel Street / one of these days.

換你朗讀。特別注意：
1. 基本原則請參考 [序2]
2. 如果需要多聽幾次示範，請到 CD-17 [00:16]
3. 請注意停頓、語氣的表現：
　　[/]：除了一般英文標點符號以外，可以停頓的地方。
　　[套色字]：加重語氣的字。

朗讀學英文 *Action*

第四步

如果需要再聽幾次，請重播 **CD-17** [00:16]

心法修練： 重播 *CD*，測驗自己習得幾成功力

Did you see that? That kid is on a suicide mission. He ____ _____ Peel Street like that every day. _____ on the fly, _____ cars, _____ curbs, _____ dogs. Sooner or later, he'll _____ and _____. He never touches the brakes. Not until he makes the bottom and then he always _____ around the corner and disappears into the traffic on Queen's Road. You watch — he'll be _____ all over Peel Street one of these days.

第五步

變化招式： 領悟基本動作的另一層意義

dodge a question 閃避問題

　　When a reporter asked the president about an unsuccessful policy, the president dodged the question by bringing up about another issue. 當記者向總統提問一個不成功的政策時，總統扯到另一個議題，藉以閃避問題。

dodge a bullet 千鈞一髮，逃過一劫

　　Candace really dodged a bullet today — she sold all her stock just minutes before the market crashed. 甘蒂絲今天真是千鈞一髮，逃過一劫——她在股市崩盤幾分鐘前，把股票都賣掉了。

40

【07】

CHOP CHOP！
切、切、切！
Kitchen Work　廚房工作

chapter 07 ▶

　　好一陣子，我白天騎腳踏車，晚上則在林記麵店打工。那是個在地下室的爛廚房，但我不介意。在林記，我學會操菜刀和切肉刀──還操得挺上手的，不過是在我不小心意外將小指頭最上面一節切掉之後。

　　For a while, I was riding my bike during the day and working at Lam's Noodles at night. It was a hellhole of a kitchen down in a basement, but I didn't mind. I learned how to handle a knife and a cleaver there —got pretty good, but not before I accidentally chopped off my little finger at the top knuckle.

來看VCR：[唐德華，廚子，林記麵店，香港，1966 年]

Billy Ho! Put that cleaver[1] down! That's not your job. Listen up. Number one, I want you to finish washing those pots. I want them <u>scrubbed[2] clean</u> and I want it done fast. Got that? Spotless. Number two, <u>haul this bucket of slop[3] out</u> and <u>dump</u> it. Number three, <u>mop up</u> that pig's blood that Little Fu just <u>spilled</u>. You've got ten minutes. Come find me when you're done and then maybe I'll let you <u>chop</u> some onions. OK, <u>let's go! Move!</u>

翻譯

　　比利·何！把切肉刀放下！那不是你的事。聽好了。第一，我要你把那些鍋子洗完。我要它們刷得乾乾淨淨的，而且你手腳要快。聽到了嗎？要清潔溜溜的。第二，把這桶餿水拿出去倒掉。第三，把小福剛打翻的豬血拖乾淨。你有十分鐘。做完後來找我，之後我搞不好會讓你切洋蔥。好，幹活去吧！去！

Word list

1. cleaver [ˈklivɚ] *n.* 切肉刀
2. scrub [skrʌb] *v.* 刷洗
3. slop [slap] *n.* 餿水

 CD-21

第一步

動作分解：跟唸 3-5 次紮實基本功

o to scrub [something] clean	把（某物）刷乾淨
o to haul [something] out	把（某物）拖出去
o to dump	倒掉
o to mop up [something]	將（某物）拭去
o to spill	使溢出
o to chop	切
o Let's go! Move!	動作快點！走！

 CD-22

第二步

發音秘笈：跟唸 2-3 次，破除你咬字含糊、發音錯誤的弱點

連音：want them >> wantem [ˋwanəm]

★ I **want them** scrubbed clean **and I want it** done fast.

請聽唐德華講這個句子，注意他將某些字連起來講的方式。每次用到連音，他就把妨礙語氣流暢的子音丟掉。講到 "want them..." 和的時候，他並沒有一字一字的說出來，而是把 want 最後的 [t] 和 them 前面的 [ð] 略過，然後將其他字串起來，變成 [wanəm]；同樣地，他把 "want it" 唸成 [wanət]。而說到 "and I..." 時，他把 and 的 [d] 略過，然後和 I 連起來唸成 [ənaɪ]。

[練習]

1. Give me two eggs **and I want them** now.
   給我兩顆蛋，我現在就要。

2. I **want a** new car **and I want it** to be red.
   我要一輛新車，而且我要紅色的。

第三步

口才練功房：重新過招，學學「唐德華」的口氣、語調

Billy Ho! Put that cleaver down! That's not your job.

Listen up. Number one, I want you to finish washing those

pots. I want them scrubbed clean / and I want it done fast.

Got that? Spotless. Number two, haul this bucket of slop out

/ and dump it. Number three, mop up that pig's blood / that

Little Fu just spilled. You've got ten minutes. Come find me

/ when you're done / and then maybe I'll let you chop some

onions. OK, let's go! Move!

換你朗讀。特別注意：

1. 基本原則請參考 [序2]

2. 如果需要多聽幾次示範，請到 CD-20 [00:05]

3. 請注意停頓、語氣的表現：

　　[/]：除了一般英文標點符號以外，可以停頓的地方。

　　[套色字]：加重語氣的字。

第四步 　　　　　　　　　　　　如果需要再聽幾次，請重播 **CD-20** [00:05]

心法修練：重播 *CD*，測驗自己習得幾成功力

　　Billy Ho! Put that cleaver down! That's not your job. Listen up. Number one, I want you to finish washing those pots. I want them _____ and I want it done fast. Got that? Spotless. Number two, _____this bucket of slop out and _____ it. Number three, _____ that pig's blood that Little Fu just _____ . You've got ten minutes. Come find me when you're done and then maybe I'll let you _____ some onions. OK, _____ ! _____ !

第五步

變化招式：領悟基本動作的另一層意義

mop up 清理；完成

　　The project is almost done, but we've still got to mop up a few things. 計畫快完成了，不過還剩幾件事情要處理。

mop the floor with someone 讓某人輸得一敗塗地

　　Jade is really good at chess. She mopped the floor with me ten games in a row. 潔德玩西洋棋真的很行，一連十局她都讓我輸得一敗塗地。

a mop of hair / mop-haired 一頭亂髮(的)

　　The mop-haired guy is John. Everyone remembers him because of his striking mop of red hair. 那個一頭亂髮的傢伙是約翰。大家都記得他，因為他有一頭搶眼的紅色亂髮。

【08】

SAVING LUCKY
拯救來福

Work and Gymnastics
工作與體操

十六歲的時候，老劉把我調到碼頭去。我或許不該談我們都在搬些什麼貨。這樣說吧，我得辭掉廚房的工作，因為我們的工作要晚上做，還要有人把風。那工作真不好做，我們得一直做到天亮，然後大伙兒在海邊一起大吃一頓。我們的酬勞是現金支付的。在我口袋裡塞著一疊鈔票，騎著腳踏車回家時，常累得像狗一樣，但是卻很快樂。

When I was sixteen, Lau moved me down to the docks. I probably shouldn't talk about the kind of cargo we were loading. Let's just say I had to quit my kitchen job because we worked at night. With a lookout. It was hard work. We worked straight through until the dawn. Then we'd all have a feast together down by the water. We got paid in cash. I rode my bike home with a wad of cash in my pocket, tired to the bone, but happy.

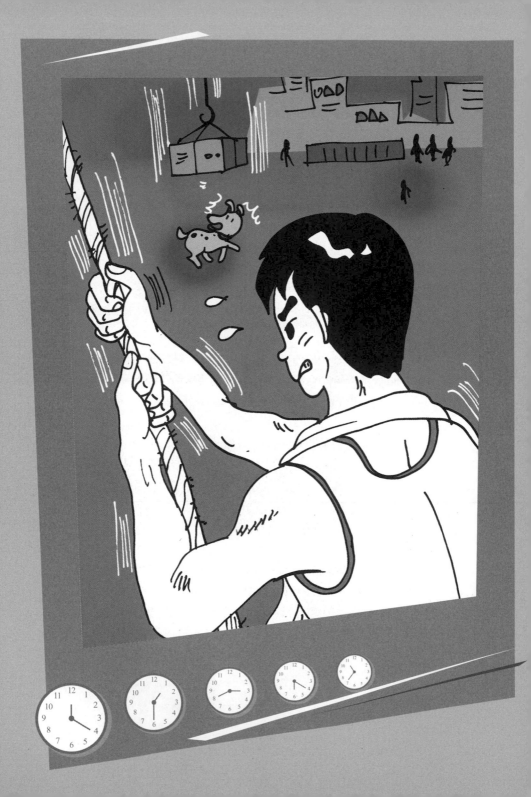

現場邀請到的是：[火腿頭山米・錢，碼頭工人]

We all liked Hatchet. He always did more than his share of work. Once, he saved Lucky's life. A pulley[1] broke loose. The crate[2] we were <u>hoisting</u>[3] down into the hold started to fall. It would've landed right on Lucky's head. Hatchet <u>caught a hold of</u> the rope and <u>yanked</u>[4] it hard to one side. The crate missed Lucky, but Hatchet <u>got dragged</u> headfirst right through the hatch. Somehow, though, he managed to <u>turn a somersault</u>[5] and <u>land on his feet</u>. He laughed about it.

翻譯

　　我們都喜歡快斧手。他總會做超過自己份內該做的事。有一次，他救了來福一命。當時滑輪斷掉脫落，原本我們慢慢往下吊的貨箱開始快速下墜，眼看著就要砸爛來福的腦袋。快斧手趕緊一把抓住繩子，往旁邊使勁一扯。箱子沒有砸到來福，倒是快斧手被拖著一頭飛出了艙口。不過他居然一個鷂子翻身，雙腳著地，毫髮無傷。事後他只是把它當笑話一則。

Word list

1. pulley [ˋpʊlɪ] *n.* 滑輪
2. crate [kret] *n.* 板條箱；竹簍
3. hoist [hɔɪst] *v.* 吊起；推舉
4. yank [jæŋk] *v.* 使勁地拉
5. somersault [ˋsʌməˌsɔlt] *n.* 翻筋斗

第一步

動作分解：跟唸 **3-5** 次紮實基本功

o to hoist	（用繩索、起重機等）吊起；提起
o to catch a hold of [something]	抓住（某物）
o to yank	使勁一扯
o to get dragged	被拖著
o to turn a somersault	翻跟斗
o to land on one's feet	雙腳著地（安然無恙）

第二步

發音秘笈：跟唸 **2-3** 次，破除你咬字含糊、發音錯誤的弱點

減化音：would've >> woulda [wʊdə]

★ It **would've** landed right on Lucky's head.

　　說英語的人士不一定會完全按照字詞原來的拼法發音。在日常用語當中，他們習慣把某些字或字組縮短、簡化。例如火腿頭把 "Would have" 縮短為 "Would've" ，並唸成 [wʊdə]。美式口語中，"Woulda"、"coulda"、"shoulda" 縮寫形式極為常見，如果不學會使用，講話反而會聽起來很造作，極不自然。

[練習]

1. If I didn't become a movie star, I **woulda** become a dance teacher.
   如果我沒有成為電影明星，我已經是一個舞蹈老師。

2. If you didn't stop me, I **woulda** hurt myself.
   如果你沒阻止我，我已經讓自己受傷了。

第三步

口才練功房：重新過招，學學「山米‧錢」的口氣、語調　CD-23

We all liked Hatchet. He always did more than his share

of work. Once, he saved Lucky's life. A pulley broke loose.

The crate we were hoisting down into the hold / started to

fall. It woulda landed right on Lucky's head. Hatchet caught

a hold of the rope and yanked it hard to one side. The crate

missed Lucky, but Hatchet got dragged headfirst right

through the hatch. Somehow, though, he managed to turn a

somersault / and land on his feet. He laughed about it.

換你朗讀。特別注意：

1. 基本原則請參考 [序2]

2. 如果需要多聽幾次示範，請到 CD-23 [00:07]

3. 請注意停頓、語氣的表現：

　[/]：除了一般英文標點符號以外，可以停頓的地方。

　[套色字]：加重語氣的字。

如果需要再聽幾次，請重播 **CD-23** [00:07]

第四步

心法修練：重播 CD，測驗自己習得幾成功力

We all liked Hatchet. He always did more than his share of work. Once, he saved Lucky's life. A pulley broke loose. The crate we were _____ down into the hold started to fall. It would've landed right on Lucky's head. Hatchet _____ the rope and _____ it hard to one side. The crate missed Lucky, but Hatchet _____ headfirst right through the hatch. Somehow, though, he managed to _____ _____ and _____ . He laughed about it.

第五步

變化招式：領悟基本動作的另一層意義

land on one's feet 安然無恙

I thought getting a divorce would destroy Bob, but he's got a new girlfriend and he's just been promoted at work. He's really landed on his feet. 我原以為離婚會毀了鮑伯，但他現在已經交了新女友，不久前還升了職。他真的已經沒事了。

think on one's feet 隨機應變

A good military leader has to be able to think on his feet in any battle situation. 無論在什麼樣的戰鬥情況下，一名優秀的軍事將領應該有隨機應變的能力。

have (got) two left feet 笨手笨腳

Did you see Martin dancing with Sally? It was really funny—she's a professional ballet dancer, and he's got two left feet. 你有沒有看到馬汀和莎莉跳舞的樣子？真好笑——女的是專業芭蕾舞家，男的卻笨手笨腳。

【09】

LOSING CHAMP
失去「冠軍」

Searching for a Cricket
尋找蟋蟀

有一天晚上，我和火腿頭山米在老劉位於旺角的一處賭場設局鬥蟋蟀。老劉有一隻特地從山東省買來的常勝軍蟋蟀，花了他八千塊港幣。如果你讓那隻蟋蟀夠餓的話，牠可是一隻兇狠的鬥蟲。老劉靠著牠，口袋裡攢進了不少銀子。不過那天晚上鬥完蟋蟀後，出了一個小麻煩。我們把「冠軍」給搞丟了。嗯，事實上比搞丟還更糟糕。

One night Ham Head Sammy and I were working a cricket fight at one of Lau's gambling dens in Mongkok. Lau had a special champion cricket from Shandong province. He paid almost $8,000 Hong Kong dollars for it. If you let it get hungry enough, that was one mean fighting bug. Mr. Lau did real good with it. But that night, after the fights, there was a little problem. We lost the Champ. Well, it was actually even worse than that.

來看VCR：[火腿頭山米．錢，蟋蟀保鑣，旺角，九龍，1976 年]

Can you see him under the bleachers[1]? <u>Get down on your hands and knees</u>, Hatchet. <u>Crawl under</u> there and look. <u>Lift up</u> that garbage — maybe he's hiding. Champ? Where are you, Champ? Sing for us, buddy. Hatchet, if we don't find him … <u>Flip</u> that board over. Be careful. Don't <u>crush</u> him, whatever you do. Oh, shit. What was that? Oh, shit. Shit! Hatchet, I really did it now. Look! I just <u>stepped on</u> the Champ. I <u>squashed</u>[2] him! He's dead, Hatchet. … He's dead — we're dead.

翻譯

　　牠有沒有在看台下面？趴下來找，快斧手。爬到那下面看看。把垃圾掀起來——搞不好牠躲在下面。冠軍！你在哪裡，冠軍？兄弟，唱個歌給我們聽聽。快斧手，要是我們找不到牠……把那塊板子翻過來。小心一點，千萬別把牠給壓扁了。哦，該死。那是什麼聲音？哦，該死。該死！快斧手，我真的完了。你看！我剛剛踩到冠軍。我把牠給踩得稀巴爛！牠死了，快斧手……牠死了——我們死定了。

Word list　1. bleacher [ˋblitʃɚ] *n.* 露天座位
　　　　　　　2. squash [skwaʃ] *v.* 壓爛

第一步

CD-27

動作分解：跟唸 **3-5** 次紮實基本功

o to get down on one's hands and knees	趴下
o to crawl under [something]	爬到（某物）底下
o to lift up [something]	抬起（某物）
o to flip [something] over	翻轉（某物）
o to crush [somthing]	壓扁（某物）
o to squash [something]	壓爛（某物）
o to step on [something]	踩到（某物）

第二步

CD-28

發音秘笈：跟唸 **2-3** 次，破除你咬字含糊、發音錯誤的弱點

自然發音：oo ＞＞ [ʊ] / [u]

★ Oh shit! **Look**! **Look** down there! ...

英文中有許多母音拼成 "oo" 的單字，例如 look、book 和 stood 等，發的是短母音 [ʊ]。許多人這個音發的不好；最常見的問題就是唸得太像長母音 [u]。記得，[ʊ] 為短母音，發音時嘴唇要放鬆，音較為短促；反之，[u] 為長母音，發音時嘴唇成圓形狀，音較長。

[練習]

| [ʊ]: | look | book | took | foot | stood |
| [u]: | loot | boot | tooth | food | shoot |

1. He **took** off his b**oo**ts. *他脫掉他的靴子。*
2. Don't sh**oo**t yourself in the f**oo**t. *不要自找麻煩。*

第三步 　CD-26

口才練功房：重新過招，學學「山米‧錢」的口氣、語調

Can you see him under the bleachers? Get down on your

hands and knees, Hatchet. Crawl under there and look. Lift

up that garbage — maybe he's hiding. Champ? Where are you,

Champ? Sing for us, buddy. Hatchet, if we don't find him …

Flip that board over. Be careful. Don't crush him, whatever

you do. Oh, shit. What was that? Oh, shit. Shit! Hatchet, I

really did it now. Look! I just stepped on the Champ. I

squashed him! He's dead, Hatchet. … He's dead — we're

dead.

換你朗讀。特別注意：

1. 基本原則請參考 [序2]

2. 如果需要多聽幾次示範，請到 CD-26 [00:06]

3. 請注意停頓、語氣的表現：

　[/]：除了一般英文標點符號以外，可以停頓的地方。

　[套色字]：加重語氣的字。

第四步

心法修練：重播 CD，測驗自己習得幾成功力

Can you see him under the bleachers? _____

_____ , Hatchet. _____ there and look. ____

____that garbage — maybe he's hiding. Champ? Where are you, Champ? Sing for us, buddy. Hatchet, if we don't find him ..._____that board over. Be careful. Don't _____ him, whatever you do. Oh, shit. What was that? Oh, shit. Shit! Hatchet, I really did it now. Look! I just _____the Champ. I _____ him! He's dead, Hatchet. ... He's dead — we're dead.

第五步

變化招式：領悟基本動作的另一層意義

flip one's lid 發怒；抓狂

When I told my sister that I'd used her toothbrush to clean my shoes, she flipped her lid. 當我跟我老姊說我用了她的牙刷來刷鞋子，她氣到抓狂。

flip-flop 突然改變心意

I wish Cary would make a final decision about which college to attend — he has flip-flopped at least four times this week. 我希望凱利可以下定決心，看到底要上哪一所大學——他這個禮拜已經反反覆覆至少四次了。

flip burgers 煎漢堡（指在速食店工作，賺微薄的辛苦錢）

My teacher told me that if I didn't study harder, I'd be flipping burgers for the rest of my life. 我的老師跟我說，如果我不用功一點，我後半輩子就得靠端盤子過活了。

【10】

RUMBA TO RIO
跳著倫巴到
里約熱內盧
Dancing 跳舞

老劉的脾氣火爆，得知冠軍的事情之後極為不悅。我覺得該是休假的時候了，於是跳上了一艘開往巴西的遊輪，喬裝成一個社交舞老師。我就這麼裝了下去。我一向步履輕盈，馬上就學會跳社交舞。不到一個禮拜，許多人已經排隊等著上我的課。抵達里約熱內盧時，我已是船上最厲害的舞者。

Lau had a real red-pepper temper and he was not happy about Champ. I decided it was time for a vacation. I jumped on a cruise ship bound for Brazil and pretended I was a ballroom dance instructor. I just faked it. I've always been light on my feet and I picked it right up. By the end of the week, they were lining up for my class. By the time we got to Rio, I was the best dancer on the ship.

來看VCR： [伊莎朵拉‧卡坎霍多，七星皇后號上的舞蹈課學生，1976 年]

Drunk? Ha! It takes more than twelve cocktails[1] to get me drunk. Mr. Ho, may I be frank? You're not the most handsome guy in the world, or even on this ship — but I find you irresistible[2]. When we dance, I feel like I'm <u>levitating</u>[3]. I feel like I'm <u>gliding on ice</u>. Please dance with me, Mr. Ho. Put one hand here... and the other... here. <u>Hold me tight</u>. <u>Swivel</u>[4] <u>your hips</u> against mine. <u>Lift me</u> and <u>spin me</u>. Dance with me, Mr. Ho. Make me happy.

翻譯

　　喝醉？哈！超過十二杯的雞尾酒我才會醉！何先生，恕我直言，你並不是全世界最帥的傢伙，甚至不是這艘船上最帥的——但我發現你的魅力無法擋。我們跳舞的時候，我覺得整個人都變得輕飄飄的，好像在冰上滑行一般。何先生，請與我共舞。把一隻手放這裡……另一隻手放……這裡。抱緊我，貼著我的臀部扭動，把我舉起來，帶著我旋轉。與我共舞，何先生，帶給我快樂吧。

Word list
1. cocktail [ˋkɑk.tel] *n.* 雞尾酒
2. irresistible [.ɪrɪˋzɪstəbl] *adj.* 不可抗拒的
3. levitate [ˋlɛvə.tet] *v.* 輕浮在空中
4. swivel [ˋswɪvl] *v.* 轉動；迴轉

CD-30

第一步

動作分解：跟唸 3-5 次紮實基本功

o to levitate	輕輕浮在空中
o to glide on ice	在冰上滑行
o to hold someone tight	抱緊某人
o to swivel one's hips	轉動臀部
o to lift someone [while dancing]	（跳舞時）舉起某人
o to spin someone [while dancing]	（跳舞時）帶著某人旋轉

第二步

CD-31

發音秘笈：跟唸 2-3 次，破除你咬字含糊、發音錯誤的弱點

停頓／語氣：

★ I feel like I'm gliding on ice. // Please dance with me.

講話時，應該適時停頓。請再聽一次伊莎朵拉的話，注意這兩句中間的聲調。伊莎朵拉請比利‧何跳舞的時候，聲調在第一個句子之後下降，稍微轉小聲，接著在停頓之後，她又提高了聲音。

[練習]

Put one hand here ... // and the other...// here. // Hold me tight. // Swivel your hips against mine. // Lift me and spin me. // Dance with me, Mr. Ho. // Make me happy.

第三步　　　　　　　　　　　　　　　　　　　　　*CD-29*

口才練功房：重新過招，學學「卡坎霍多」的口氣、語調

Drunk? Ha! It takes more than twelve cocktails to get me drunk. Mr. Ho, may I be frank? You're not the most handsome guy in the world, or even on this ship — but I find you irresistible. When we dance, I feel like I'm levitating. I feel like I'm gliding on ice. Please dance with me, Mr. Ho. Put one hand here... and the other... here. Hold me tight. Swivel your hips against mine. Lift me and spin me. Dance with me, Mr. Ho. Make me happy.

換你朗讀。特別注意：

1. 基本原則請參考 [序2]

2. 如果需要多聽幾次示範，請到 CD-29 [00:06]

3. 請注意停頓、語氣的表現：

　[/]：除了一般英文標點符號以外，可以停頓的地方。

　[套色字]：加重語氣的字。

心法修練：重播 *CD*，測驗自己習得幾成功力

如果需要再聽幾次，請重播 **CD-29** [00:06]

Drunk? Ha! It takes more than twelve cocktails to get me drunk. Mr. Ho, may I be frank? You're not the most handsome guy in the world, or even on this ship—but I find you irresistible. When we dance, I feel like I'm _____. I feel like I'm _____. Please dance with me, Mr. Ho. Put one hand here ... and the other ... here. _____. _____ against mine. _____ and _____. Dance with me, Mr. Ho. Make me happy.

變化招式：領悟基本動作的另一層意義

spin a story 編造故事

The president was caught in a dark room with his secretary. The White House will probably spin the story like this: the president was just encouraging his staff to save electricity. 總統被撞見在昏暗的房間中和秘書瞎搞。白宮八成會如此編造故事：總統只不過是在鼓勵職員省電。

someone's head is spinning 某人感到暈頭轉向

I have no idea what I'm going to do with the $100,000,000 I won in the lottery. My head's spinning—I still can't believe I'm rich! 我不知道該怎麼處置我玩樂透贏的一億美元。我的頭都昏了──我還是不敢相信我致富了！

spin one's wheels 空轉；原地踏步

I've got to get a new job. Nobody notices anything I do for this company—I'm just spinning my wheels here. 我得找一份新工作。在這家公司中根本沒有人在注意我做了什麼──在這裡我不過是在空轉罷了。

Bill in Brazil
在巴西的日子

比利，顯然你天生就充滿了運動細胞。你是個武術家和雜技表演家。你也是位有才華的動作諧星，以不怕死、創意十足的特技聲名大噪。聽說你還是個很好的交際舞蹈家呢。你是怎麼激發你的才華，發展出那麼多技藝的？你還受過哪些特殊訓練？有沒有任何特別的良師指導你？你在巴西是不是真的學過柔術？告訴我們一些動作明星必須接受的養成訓練吧。

Billy, you've obviously got a lot of natural athletic talent. You're a martial artist and an acrobat. You're a gifted physical comedian and famous for your daring, inventive stunt work. I hear you're even a pretty good ballroom dancer. How did you go about honing your talent and developing all those skills? What sort of special training did you have? Did you have any special mentors? Is it true that you learned Jiujitsu in Brazil? Tell us a little bit about the education of an action star.

【11】
BEAT UP IN BRAZIL
在巴西遭海扁
Wrestling 摔角

我並沒有預先訓練些什麼,碰到什麼我就學什麼。我是這麼學會跳舞的,也是這麼學會打鬥的。我到巴西的第一天,就在一家酒吧裡被一個綜合武術搏鬥家打得落花流水。他把我打倒在地上,還把我像麻花一樣五花大綁起來。我對摔角一竅不通,所以我每天晚上回到同一家酒吧,找那個傢伙打一場架,一直到學會為止。

I don't really train ahead of time for anything. I learn as I go. That's how I learned to dance. That's how I learned to fight, too. My first day in Brazil, I got beat up in a bar by a vale tudo fighter. He knocked me down and tied me up like a pretzel on the floor. I didn't know anything about wrestling. So I went back to that same bar every night and picked a fight with that same guy until I learned.

chapter 11

現場邀請到的是：[賈凡‧迪奧達多，格鬥家]

He just kept coming. The whole neighborhood showed up to watch. People started to bet on how long he would last. I used a dozen different submission[1] holds on him. I <u>wrenched</u>[2] his knees and his ankles. I <u>bent</u> his arms. I <u>choked</u> him. He wouldn't quit. Finally, to get rid of him, I <u>broke</u> a couple of his fingers. But he was right back the next night. They <u>cheered for him</u> that night. That's when I realized that, sooner or later, he would beat[3] me.

翻譯

　　他一再地找上門，附近所有的人都跑來看。大家開始打起賭來，想看他能撐多久。我對他用了十幾種不同的制服招數。我絞他的膝蓋和腳踝，扳他的手臂，招他的喉嚨，他就是不認輸。最後為了擺脫他，我弄斷了他幾根手指頭。不過隔晚他又現身。那天晚上，大家都為他加油打氣。就在那一刻我領悟到，遲早他會打敗我。

Word list | 1. submission [səbˋmɪʃən] n. 降服 　　3. beat [bit] v. 打敗
| 2. wrench [rɛntʃ] v. 用力扭轉

第一步

動作分解：跟唸 **3-5** 次紮實基本功

o to wrench [someone's knees/ankles]	絞（某人的膝蓋 / 腳踝）
o to bend [someone's arms]	扳（某人的手臂）
o to choke someone	招某人喉嚨
o to break [someone's fingers]	折斷（某人的手指頭）
o to cheer for someone	為某人歡呼

第二步

發音秘笈：跟唸 **2-3** 次，破除你咬字含糊、發音錯誤的弱點

減化音： wouldn't ≫ wouldn('t)

★ He **wouldn't** quit.

英語人士平常講話使用縮減法時，經常會把字詞最後的子音省略掉。賈凡並沒有清楚的把 "Wouldn't" 後面的 [t] 音發出來，但是他的舌頭其實是放在發 [t] 音的位置上，只是沒有真正發出音來而已："He wouldn ('t) quit." [t] 音當然可以清楚地唸出來，但是在英文口語當中，輕鬆的減化音是比較常見的。

[練習]

1. I **woundn('t)** do that if I were you.
   如果我是你我不會這樣做。

2. They said they **wouldn('t)** let me do my own stunts.
   他們說不會讓我做我想做的特技。

口才練功房：重新過招，學學「迪奧達多」的口氣、語調

He just kept coming. The whole neighborhood showed up to watch. People started to bet / on how long he would last. I used a dozen different submission holds on him. I wrenched his knees and his ankles. I bent his arms. I choked him. He wouldn't quit. Finally, to get rid of him, I broke a couple of his fingers. But he was right back the next night. They cheered for him that night. That's when I realized that, sooner or later, he would beat me.

換你朗讀。特別注意：

1. 基本原則請參考 [序2]

2. 如果需要多聽幾次示範，請到 CD-32 [00:20]

3. 請注意停頓、語氣的表現：

[/]：除了一般英文標點符號以外，可以停頓的地方。

[套色字]：加重語氣的字。

第四步　　　　　　　　　　　　　如果需要再聽幾次，請重播 CD-32 [00:20]

心法修練： 重播 CD，測驗自己習得幾成功力

He just kept coming. The whole neighborhood showed up to watch. People started to bet on how long he would last. I used a dozen different submission holds on him. I ＿＿＿＿ his knees and his ankles. I ＿＿＿＿ his arms. I ＿＿＿＿ him. He wouldn't quit. Finally, to get rid of him, I ＿＿＿＿ a couple of his fingers. But he was right back the next night. They ＿＿＿＿ that night. That's when I realized that, sooner or later, he would beat me.

第五步

變化招式： 領悟基本動作的另一層意義

wrench one's ankle/wrist/shoulder/knee
扭傷腳踝／手腕／肩膀／膝蓋

I can't play football this weekend—I wrenched my knee while running down the stairs yesterday. 這個週末我不能打橄欖球了——昨天跑下樓梯的時候，我扭傷了膝蓋。

gut-wrenching 感人肺腑的

The suicide scene of the movie of *Romeo and Juliet* was so gut-wrenching that I'll never forget it. 電影《羅密歐與茱麗葉》中自殺的那一幕真是感人肺腑，我永遠也忘不了。

throw a (monkey) wrench into the works 使順利進行的事受阻撓

John quit yesterday?! That really throws a wrench into the works—how will we ever finish the project on time without him? 約翰昨天辭職了！？這會把事情搞砸的——沒有他，我們的計畫要怎麼如期完成呢？

[12]

ON (AND OFF) THE ROAD TO PARÁ

到帕拉沿途的經歷

Driving 開車

　　我也是這樣學會了開車——在工作時學會的。我和賈凡打過好多次架，後來竟變成了朋友。他找到人雇用我們開卡車到巴西北部，到位於帕拉的一座金礦。出發後第一天晚上夜深的時候，輪到了我開車，我只得跟他說我從來沒有開過車。他說：「開車不難，你會找出訣竅的。」說了就倒頭大睡，但並沒睡太久。

I learned to drive the same way — on the job. Djavan and I fought so many times, we became friends. He got us hired to drive a truck to the north of Brazil, to a gold mine in Pará. Late the first night out, when it was my turn to take over at the wheel, I had to tell him I'd never driven before. He said, "It's not hard. You'll figure it out." Then he fell asleep. He wasn't asleep for very long.

chapter 12

來看VCR：[賈凡・迪奧達多，二號高速公路，巴伊亞，巴西，1976 年]

Did we just <u>run over</u> a tree? Ho? Where's the road? Whoa! Watch out! <u>Crank</u>[1] it left! No! The *other* left! OK, you just killed a goat. At least you <u>used your turn signal</u>. Don't feel bad—we'll eat him. Let's just <u>slow down</u> and see if we can find the road. Now just <u>brake</u>, nice and easy. Uh, no—not *that* one. You're <u>pressing on the gas</u>. I'm going to <u>shift</u> you into neutral[2]. Ho? That's a river. Please <u>hit the brakes</u>. Anytime now.

翻譯

　　我們剛剛是不是輾過了一棵樹？小何？馬路呢？喔！小心！方向盤打左！不！是**另一個**左邊！好，你剛剛撞死了一隻山羊。至少你打了方向燈。別難過——我們可以吃了牠。我們開慢一點，看看找不找得到馬路。現在踩煞車，慢慢來，輕輕的。呃，不——不是踩**哪裡**。你踩的是**油門**。我要幫你換到空檔。小何？那裡是河。請你踩煞車。現在就踩。

Word list　| 1. crank [kræŋk] *v.* 轉動曲柄
　　　　　　　| 2. neutral [ˈnutrəl] *n.* 空檔

第一步

動作分解： 跟唸 3-5 次紮實基本功

o to run over [something]	輾過（某物）
o to crank [a steering wheel]	突然轉動（方向盤）
o to use the turn signal	打方向燈
o to slow down	放慢速度
o to brake	用煞車（減速或停住）
o to press on the gas	踩油門
o to shift [the gears of a car]	換（車檔）
o to hit the brakes	猛踩煞車

第二步

發音秘笈： 跟唸 2-3 次，破除你咬字含糊、發音錯誤的弱點

加強語氣：

★ Uh, no —not *that* one. You're pressing on the *gas*.

聽聽賈凡如何加強 **that** 和 **gas** 的語氣。縱使他急著要說比利・何踩的是油門，但他為了強調那兩個字而放慢了速度。試試這兩種方法，速度加快和放慢，你會發現要強調某個字的時候，說話速度放慢一點點效果比較好。同時，想強調某個字時你也可以大聲一點地說，必要的時候甚至可以非常大聲地說出來。

[練習]
1. No, no, no — not a *boat*. I ran over a *goat*.
   不，不，不——不是船，我輾過的是一隻山羊。
2. I said turn *right*, not *left*.
   我是說轉右邊，不是左邊。

第三步

口才練功房：重新過招，學學「迪奧達多」的口氣、語調

Did we just run over a tree? Ho? Where's the road?

Whoa! Watch out! Crank it left! No! The *other* left! OK, you

just killed a goat. At least you used your turn signal. Don't

feel bad — we'll eat him. Let's just slow down / and see if we

can find the road. Now just brake, nice and easy. Uh, no—not

that one. You're pressing on the *gas*. I'm going to shift you

into neutral. Ho? That's a river. Please hit the brakes.

Anytime now.

換你朗讀。特別注意：
1. 基本原則請參考 [序2]
2. 如果需要多聽幾次示範，請到 CD-35 [00:28]
3. 請注意停頓、語氣的表現：
　　[/]：除了一般英文標點符號以外，可以停頓的地方。
　　[套色字]：加重語氣的字。

77

第四步

如果需要再聽幾次，請重播CD-35[00:28]

心法修練：重播CD，測驗自己習得幾成功力

Did we just _____ a tree? Ho? Where's the road? Whoa! Watch out! _____ it left! No! The *other* left! OK, you just killed a goat. At least you _____. Don't feel bad—we'll eat him. Let's just _____ and see if we can find the road. Now just _____, nice and easy. Uh, no—not *that* one. You're _____ _____. I'm going to _____ you into neutral. Ho? That's a river. Please _____. Anytime now.

第五步

變化招式：領悟基本動作的另一層意義

run up a considerable/large/huge bill
積欠滿大／很大／非常大的一筆債

　　While I was on vacation, I ran up a huge credit card bill. 度假的時候，我刷信用卡，積了一大筆卡債。

runaway 失控的

　　The biggest economic problem is runaway inflation, just as the most frightening traffic problem is a runaway car. 最嚴重的經濟問題就是失控的通貨膨脹，正如最可怕的交通問題就是失控的汽車。

run away from home 逃家／runway 逃走的人

　　I didn't run away from home— I'm no runaway. 我沒有逃家——我可不是蹺家的人。

【13】

BACKCOUNTRY GYM
荒野健身

Exercise Regime 運動習慣

　　巴西是個幅員遼闊的地方，開車到培拉達山的金礦得花不少時間。坐著不動簡直要把我逼瘋了，於是我訂下一個健身計劃。每開一英哩，我就做一次伏地挺身和一次仰臥起坐。我們每開二百英哩休息一次，我和賈凡就一起健身。直到今天，我都還有這個習慣。我是說，白天時我經常會放下手邊的事，就地做他個二百下伏地挺身和二百下仰臥起坐。

chapter 13 ▶

　　Brazil is a big place. Driving to the gold mine in Serra Pelada took a long time. Sitting still was driving me crazy, so I made up an exercise program. For every mile we drove, I did one push-up and one sit-up. We'd stop every two hundred miles and Djavan and I would do the workout together. To this day, I still have that habit. I mean, every so often during the day I'll just drop down and do 200 push-ups and 200 sit-ups.

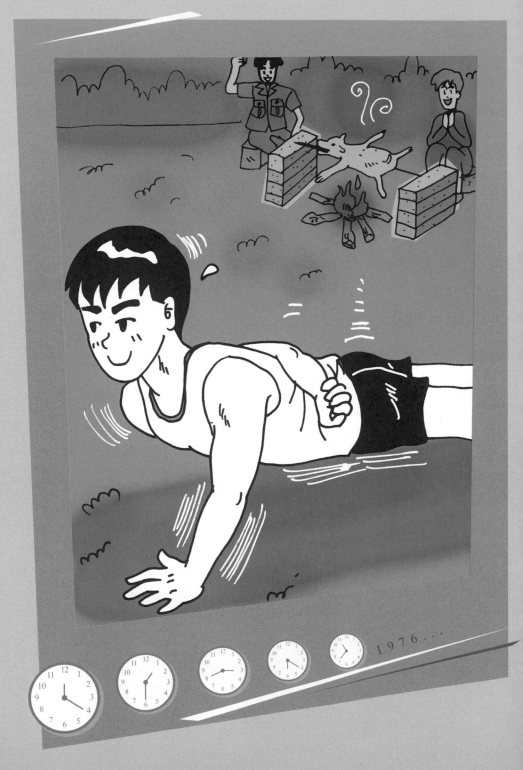

來看VCR：[達爾米拉‧蒙帝，搭便車的少年，帕拉州，巴西，1976 年]

Hey, thanks guys! This roasted goat is good. Real tasty. What're you <u>doing sit-ups</u> for? Are you guys soldiers? My uncle is in the army. He <u>lifts weights</u>. We're not driving to a war, are we? Hey—you're supposed to[1] <u>keep your back straight</u> when you <u>do push-ups</u>. I bet you can't <u>push yourself up off the ground</u> and <u>clap your hands</u>. OK—I was wrong. I bet you can't <u>do a one-arm push-up</u>. OK—I was wrong. Anyway, mind if I have another piece of goat?

翻譯

　　嘿，謝謝你們啦！這烤山羊真棒，好吃極了。你們做伏地挺身幹嘛？你們是軍人嗎？我舅舅在軍中服役，他練的是舉重。我們該不會是開車去打仗吧，嗯？嘿──伏地挺身的時候，你應該要把背挺直。我打賭你沒辦法把身體挺離地面，然後雙手擊掌。好吧──我錯了。我打賭你不會單手做伏地挺身。好吧──我錯了。不管怎樣，介意我再吃一塊羊肉嗎？

Word list ∣ 1. be supposed to 被認為應該……

第一步

動作分解：跟唸 3-5 次紮實基本功

o to do sit-ups	做仰臥起坐
o to lift weights	舉重
o to keep one's back straight	將背挺直
o to do push-ups	做伏地挺身
o to push oneself up off the ground	把身體挺離地面
o to clap one's hands	擊掌；拍手
o to do a one-arm push-up	單手做扶地挺身

第二步

發音秘笈：跟唸 2-3 次，破除你咬字含糊、發音錯誤的弱點

減化音與連音：you're supposed to >> yer sposta
[jɚsə`postə]

★ Hey — **you're supposed to** keep your back straight...

口語英文中，原本應該分開的字詞經常會連在一起說，有時是二字甚至三字以上串在一起唸，完全不分開。聽不慣英文的人，可能會以為聽到的是一個單字。"you're supposed to..." yer sposta：[jɚsə`postə]。"you're" 和 "to" 被減化後成了 [jɚ] 和 [tə]，而 supposed 最後一個字母 d 則和 to 開頭的 t 連在一起成為一個音。

[練習]
1. **Yer sposta** be tough. 你應該要強硬點。
2. **Yer sposta** duck before I swing. 你應該在我揮拳前躲開。

第三步

CD-38

口才練功房：重新過招，學學「蒙帝」的口氣、語調

Hey, thanks guys! This roasted goat is good. Real tasty.

What're you doing sit-ups for? Are you guys soldiers? My

uncle is in the army. He lifts weights. We're not driving to a

war, are we? Hey—yer sposta keep your back straight / when

you do push-ups. I bet you can't push yourself up off the

ground / and clap your hands. OK—I was wrong. I bet you

can't do a one-arm push-up. OK—I was wrong. Anyway, mind

if I have another piece of goat?

換你朗讀。特別注意：
1. 基本原則請參考 [序2]
2. 如果需要多聽幾次示範，請到 CD-38 [00:07]
3. 請注意停頓、語氣的表現：
　　[/]：除了一般英文標點符號以外，可以停頓的地方。
　　[⌒]：特殊音調上揚或下降。
　　[套色字]：加重語氣的字。

第四步

如果需要再聽幾次，請重播 CD-38 [00:07]

心法修練：重播CD，測驗自己習得幾成功力

Hey, thanks guys! This roasted goat is good. Real tasty. What're you _____ for? Are you guys soldiers? My uncle is in the army. He _____. We're not driving to a war, are we? Hey — you're supposed to _____ when you _____. I bet you can't _____ and _____. OK — I was wrong. I bet you can't _____. OK — I was wrong. Anyway, mind if I have another piece of goat?

第五步

變化招式：領悟基本動作的另一層意義

not lift a finger (to help someone) 連根手指都不抬一下；一點事都不做

　　You should be ashamed of yourself — you watched your wife change a tire on your car and didn't lift a finger to help her. What kind of husband are you, anyway? 你應該感到羞愧——就這麼看著你老婆換車輪胎，你卻連一根手指頭都懶得抬一下。你這算是哪門子的丈夫啊？

give someone a lift 載某人一程

　　You're going to the library? Can you give me a lift? I'd really appreciate it. 你要去圖書館嗎？可不可以載我一程？我會非常感激的。

give someone a lift / lift someone's spirits 鼓舞某人；振奮某人

　　A few words of praise from my boss really lifted my spirits. She really gave me a lift at a difficult time. 我老闆幾句讚美的話真的讓我精神為之一振。在困難的時候，她的話真的鼓舞了我。

【14】

SERRA PELADA
培拉達山

Acrobatics 雜技表演

　　到了培拉達山，我和賈凡決定在金礦區試試自己的運氣。那礦坑是個又大又深又醜的洞，你得爬下十幾個不同的木梯才到得了底部。在那裡比在林記麵店工作更糟，不過我不介意。為了娛樂自己，我在梯子上自創了幾種把戲。我和賈凡也會藉討論如果我們找到一大塊金子，會舉辦什麼樣的大派對來打發時間。但我們並沒有找到多少金子。

　　At Serra Pelada Djavan and I decided to try our luck at the gold mine. It was a huge, deep, ugly hole in the ground. You had to climb down a dozen different wooden ladders to get to the bottom. It was even worse than working at Lam's Noodles, but I didn't mind. To amuse myself, I made up tricks on the ladders. Djavan and I passed the time talking about the huge party we'd throw if we ever found a big nugget of gold. But we never did find much gold.

來看VCR：[阿多爾朶・達・羅沙，採礦工，培拉達山，
巴西，1976 年]

You guys don't believe me? Let's put some money on it. One hundred cruzeiros[1] says the Chinese kid can <u>climb a ladder backwards</u>. I've seen him <u>swing like a monkey</u> from one ladder, <u>fly through the air</u> and <u>land on</u> another. He can <u>run up </u>a ladder with no hands. He can <u>balance</u>[2] a ladder straight up in the air, run up it, and <u>do a hand-stand</u>[3] on the top of the poles. You don't believe it? I'll go find him. Get your money out.

翻譯

你們大夥不相信我？咱們來賭點錢。跟你們賭一百克魯賽羅，這中國小子可以倒著爬梯子。我看過他像猴子一樣從一個梯子盪過半空到另一個梯子上。他上梯子還可以不用手。他可以把梯子直立起來，保持平衡，爬上梯子，然後在頂端做倒立。你們不相信？我這就去找他。把你們的錢掏出來。

Word list | 1. cruzeiro [kruˋzero] *n.*（巴西幣值）克魯塞羅
 | 2. balance [ˋbæləns] *v.* 平衡
 | 3. handstand [ˋhænd͵stænd] *n.* 倒立

CD-42

第一步

動作分解：跟唸 3-5 次紮實基本功

o to climb [something backwards]	（在某物上倒著）攀爬
o to swing [like a monkey]	（像猴子一樣）擺盪
o to fly through the air	飛躍過半空
o to land [on something]	降落（在某物上）
o to run up a ladder	上梯子
o to balance something	平衡某物
o to do a handstand	做倒立

第二步

CD-43

發音秘笈：跟唸 2-3 次，破除你咬字含糊、發音錯誤的弱點

舉一連串動作或東西

★ I've seen him **swing** like a monkey from **one** ladder, **fly** through the **air**, and **land** on **another**.

在句子中，加重某些字的語氣，有助於釐清語意。聽聽達·羅沙先生如何描述比利·何，從他說話的語調，我們可以很清楚地知道，他是在列舉比利會做的特技（盪、飛躍、降落），兩種相關的事物（猴子和半空中），以及特技發生的兩個地點（兩個不同的梯子）。如果你在一個句子裡要列舉一連串動作或東西，試試模仿達·羅沙的語氣。

[練習]
1. Billy likes to **run 20** miles, **do 200** push-ups and then **have** a **light** breakfast. 比利喜歡跑20英哩、做200下扶地挺身，然後吃一份清淡的早餐。
2. He usually **punches** his opponent in the **stomach**, then **knees** him in the **groin**, and then **smiles** before **hitting** him in the **face**. 他通常會揍對手的肚子、踢他跨下，然後笑一笑，再賞他的臉一拳。

第三步

口才練功房：重新過招，學學「達‧羅沙」的口氣、語調

You guys don't believe me? Let's put some money on it.

One hundred cruzeiros / says the Chinese kid can climb a ladder backwards. I've seen him swing like a monkey from one ladder, fly through the air / and land on another. He can run up a ladder with no hands. He can balance a ladder / straight up in the air, run up it, and do a handstand / on the top of the poles. You don't believe it? I'll go find him. Get your money out.

換你朗讀。特別注意：

1. 基本原則請參考 [序2]

2. 如果需要多聽幾次示範，請到 CD-41 [00:06]

3. 請注意停頓、語氣的表現：

　　[/]：除了一般英文標點符號以外，可以停頓的地方。

　　[套色字]：加重語氣的字。

如果需要再聽幾次，請重播 **CD-41** [00:06]

第四步

心法修練：重播CD，測驗自己習得幾成功力

You guys don't believe me? Let's put some money on it. One hundred cruzeiros says the Chinese kid can _____. I've seen him _____ from one ladder, _____ and _____ another. He can _____ ladder with no hands. He can _____ a ladder straight up in the air, run up it, and _____ _____ on the top of the poles. You don't believe it? I'll go find him. Get your money out.

第五步

變化招式：領悟基本動作的另一層意義

hang in the balance 安危未卜

　　The fire-fighters raced against time to put out the raging house fire. The lives of three small children hung in the balance. 消防員與時間賽跑，試圖撲滅屋裡猛烈的大火。三名幼兒的性命安危未卜。

balance the books / balance your checkbook 平衡銀行帳戶收支

　　If you never balance your checkbook, how do you know how much money you have left in your account? 如果你從不計算銀行帳戶的收支，怎麼知道帳戶裡剩多少錢？

fair and balanced 公正、平衡的

　　The media should try to give fair and balanced reports, not polemical arguments. 媒體應該提供公正、平衡的報導，而不是充滿辯證意味的論點。

【15】

CIRCUS 馬戲團
Pratfalls 摔跤搞笑

在 1977 年的元旦那天，有一個巡迴演出的馬戲團前來為礦工表演。大夥都愛死了。馬戲團裡有一個小丑會吐火，還兩個美麗的女孩子，只需花幾個克魯賽羅就能和她們跳舞。幾名礦工說服我表演我的梯子把戲給群眾看。馬戲團團長看了很佩服，想給我一份工作。我說：「你可不可以也雇用巴西最好的摔角選手賈凡‧迪奧達多？」他說可以，於是我們就加入了馬戲團。

On New Year's Day, 1977, a traveling circus came to perform for the miners. We all loved it. They had a clown who could breathe fire and they had two beautiful girls you could dance with for a few cruzeiros. Some of the miners talked me into doing some of my ladder tricks for the crowd. The circus owner was so impressed, he offered me a job. I said, "Will you also take Djavan Deodato the Best Wrestler in Brazil?" He said yes, so we joined the circus.

來看VCR：[傑圖里奧・克普，馬戲團團長，在巴西貝林郊外紮營，1977 年]

Ho, you're too good. You need to add a bit of suspense[1] to your act. When you come out with the ladder, <u>stumble[2]</u> a bit. Make 'em believe you might <u>trip and fall</u>. Pretend[3] you're gonna <u>drop</u> the ladder on 'em. When you're climbing, let yourself <u>slip</u>. When you're up top and you start walking the ladder, <u>swerve[4] and wobble[5]</u> and <u>make it dip</u>. You might <u>take a tumble</u> or two. No problem. It's acting. Make 'em believe you might fail, then wow 'em.

翻譯

　　小何，你太厲害了。你得在表演中吊一下觀眾的胃口。當你拿著梯子出場的時候，稍微跟蹌一下，讓他們以為你會絆倒。假裝你的梯子會掉下來壓到他們。爬梯子的時候，讓自己踩個空。上到頂端開始踩梯子走的時候，要左搖右晃，讓梯子傾斜一下。你可以跌個一兩次，沒問題，演戲嘛。讓觀眾以為你會跌落，然後聽他們「哇！哇！」地驚呼。

Word list	
1. suspense [sə`spɛns] *n.* 懸疑；擔心	4. swerve [swɜv] *v.* 偏離
2. stumble [`stʌmb!] *v.* 跟蹌	5. wobble [`wab!] *v.* 搖晃
3. pretend [prɪ`tɛnd] *v.* 假裝	

朗讀學英文 Action

第一步 CD-45

動作分解：跟唸 3-5 次紮實基本功

o to stumble	跟蹌；絆腳
o to trip and fall	絆到；摔倒
o to drop [something]	失手掉落（某物）
o to slip	滑跤
o to swerve and wobble	偏離方向，搖搖晃晃
o to make something dip	讓某物傾斜
o to take a tumble	跌跤；摔倒

第二步 CD-46

發音秘笈：跟唸 2-3 次，破除你咬字含糊、發音錯誤的弱點

加強語氣：

★ When you come **out** with the ladder, **stumble** a bit.

馬戲團團長傑圖里奧‧克普講到 stumble 一詞時加強了語氣。講到某個動作的時候，加強語氣是很普遍的作法。不過克普也強調句子第一部份中的 out 一詞，卻沒有強調 come。為什麼呢？因為方向在這個動詞片語中比較重要。當我們說 "Come in" 或 "Come out" 時，重點是方向，不是動作。請聽以下動詞片語的唸法；注意重音都在表方向的副詞上，不在動詞：

[練習]

1. After you come **in** from the patio, **close** the window.
   你從陽台上進來後，關上窗。

2. After you get **in**, **pause** a bit.
   你進來後，停頓一下。

第三步 *CD-44*

口才練功房：重新過招，學學「克普」的口氣、語調

Ho, you're too good. You need to add a little bit of suspense to your act. When you come out with the ladder, stumble a bit. Make 'em believe you might trip and fall. Pretend you're gonna drop the ladder on 'em. When you're climbing, let yourself slip. When you're up top / and you start walking the ladder, swerve and wobble / and make it dip. You might take a tumble or two. No problem. It's acting. Make 'em believe you might fail, then wow 'em.

換你朗讀。特別注意：

1. 基本原則請參考 [序2]

2. 如果需要多聽幾次示範，請到 CD-44 [00:05]

3. 請注意停頓、語氣的表現：

   [/]：除了一般英文標點符號以外，可以停頓的地方。

   [套色字]：加重語氣的字。

如果需要再聽幾次，請重播 CD-44 [00:05]

第四步

心法修練：重播 CD，測驗自己習得幾成功力

Ho, you're too good. You need to add a bit of suspense to your act. When you come out with the ladder, _____ a bit. Make 'em believe you might _____ . Pretend you're gonna _____ the ladder on 'em. When you're climbing, let yourself _____ . When you're up top and you start walking the ladder, _____ and _____ . You might _____ or two. No problem. It's acting. Make 'em believe you might fail, then wow 'em.

第五步

變化招式：領悟基本動作的另一層意義

one's grades/performance/concentration slip(s)
成績／表現／注意力下滑變差

My teacher warned me that my grades have been slipping, so I need to study harder. 我的老師警告我，我的成績一直不斷下滑，所以必須更用功。

slip someone something / slip something to someone
偷偷塞給某人某物

Jane's mother said that Jane couldn't have any money for shopping, but her father slipped her some cash before she left. What a nice dad! 珍的媽媽說不准給珍任何錢買東西，但珍出門之前，她爸爸卻偷偷塞了一些現金給她。真是個好爸爸！

slip in/out 溜進／溜出

The bank robbers slipped in and slipped out without the bank's guards noticing. 竊賊溜進又溜出，銀行警衛絲毫沒有察覺。

Ho on Health
比利・何的
健康寶典

　　比利，你在最新電影當中有一些非常驚人的特技表演。那個一路從竹子搭的鷹架上嘩啦啦地摔下來的人真的是你嗎？哎唷！看起來真的很痛！儘管受過不少重傷，你依舊結實、俐落。你的手腳好像只有你年紀一半的人。你是怎麼辦到的？有沒有特殊的飲食？專屬的醫生？你的秘訣是什麼？

　　Billy, you do some amazing acrobatic stunts in your latest movie. Was that really you crashing through that bamboo scaffolding? Ouch! That looked like it really hurt! Despite having suffered a number of serious injuries, you're still fit and nimble. You move like a man half your age. How do you do it? Do you have a special diet? A special doctor? What's your secret?

【16】

GUSTATORY GUSTO 飲食嗜好
Playing with Food 耍弄食物

　　我沒有什麼健康秘訣。我餓了就吃，累了就睡，其他時間就一直不停的動。幾年前，有幾個生意人想幫我出健康和運動的錄影帶，說什麼大家都會聽我的建議掏出大把的鈔票。真是滿嘴狗屁。我這就跟你們說說如何維持健康，而且免錢。不要老是坐著，站起來，讓屁股離開椅子，做點事，然後吃東西，再睡他一覺。就這麼簡單。

　　I don't have any health secrets. When I'm hungry, I eat. When I'm tired, I sleep. The rest of the time, I keep moving. A couple years ago, some businessmen wanted me to make a health and exercise video. They said people would pay big money for my advice. What a load of horse hooey. Here's my advice for good health and you can have it for free. Don't sit around. Get up off your butt. Do something. After that, eat. After that, sleep. That's it.

現場邀請到的是：[歐佩佩，三角點心茶樓老闆娘，九龍]

When he was a young man, Billy used to eat here every Saturday, at dawn, with the other dock workers. He had a special trick[1] he used to do to impress[2] his friends. He'd <u>take a sharpened chopstick in each hand</u>. Then he'd start <u>spearing</u>[3] stuff—shrimp rolls, pork dumplings, you name it— and he'd <u>flip it all up in the air</u>, like he was <u>juggling</u>[4]. But the food never came back down. He'd <u>catch it in his mouth</u> and <u>gulp</u>[5] it down.

翻譯

　　在比利還是個年輕小伙子的時候，每個星期六，天剛亮時，會和其他碼頭工人一起來這裡吃飯。他常耍一個特別的把戲，讓他的朋友都很佩服。他會兩手各握一根削尖的筷子，然後開始把食物叉起來——蝦捲、豬肉餃子，什麼都叉——接著把東西往空中一拋，像是在玩雜耍。但是食物從來不會掉下來，因為他會用嘴巴接住，一口吞下肚。

Word list

1. trick [trɪk] *n.* 把戲
2. impress [ɪm`prɛs] *v.* 讓（人）印象深刻
3. spear [spɪr] *v.* （以尖物）刺
4. juggle [`dʒʌgl] *v.* （將手中物件輪流拋上半空中）雜耍
5. gulp [gʌlp] *v.* 大口吞

第一步

動作分解：跟唸 3-5 次紮實基本功

o to take something in one's hand 　　用手握住某物

o to spear [something] 　　戳（某物）

o to flip something up into the air 　　把某物拋向空中

o to juggle 　　雙手輪流丟物雜耍

o to catch [something in one's mouth] （用嘴巴將某物）接住

o to gulp something down 　　吞嚥某物

第二步

發音秘笈：跟唸 2-3 次，破除你咬字含糊、發音錯誤的弱點

單音節字串：

★ He'd **flip** it **all up** in the **air**.

　　一連串單音節的字在一起有時比一個很長的單字還難流暢地說出來。這是因為多音節單字有很清楚的發音標準，字典都會標示出重音節的所在。反觀單音節的詞串，由於每個字只有一個音節，重音究竟該放在哪裡很難判斷。一般而言，名詞 (air)、動詞 (flip)、形容詞 (all) 和副詞 (up) 等所謂「實詞」要重讀。反之，代名詞、介詞、冠詞和助動詞等「虛詞」則輕讀。請聽下面的句子：

[練習]

1. He'd **catch** it in his **mouth** and **gulp** it **down**.

　　他會用嘴巴接住，一口吞下肚。

2. She'd **toss** it **up** and **out** and **kick** it **far**.

　　她會丟得高高的，然後一腳把它踢的老遠。

第三步

口才練功房：重新過招，學學「歐佩佩」的口氣、語調

CD-47

When he was a young man, Billy used to eat here every Saturday, at dawn, with the other dock workers. He had a special trick / he used to do / to impress his friends. He'd take a sharpened chopstick in each hand. Then he'd start spearing stuff — shrimp rolls, pork dumplings, you name it — and he'd flip it all up in the air, like he was juggling. But the food never came back down. He'd catch it in his mouth / and gulp it down.

換你朗讀。特別注意：

1. 基本原則請參考 [序2]

2. 如果需要多聽幾次示範，請到 CD-47 [00:22]

3. 請注意停頓、語氣的表現：

　　[/]：除了一般英文標點符號以外，可以停頓的地方。

　　[套色字]：加重語氣的字。

第四步　　　　　　　　　　如果需要再聽幾次，請重播CD-47 [00:22]

心法修練：重播CD，測驗自己習得幾成功力

When he was a young man, Billy used to eat here every Saturday, at dawn, with the other dock workers. He had a special trick he used to do to impress his friends. He'd ＿＿＿＿＿＿＿

＿＿＿＿＿ . Then he'd start ＿＿＿＿＿ stuff—shrimp rolls, pork dumplings, you name it— and he'd ＿＿＿＿＿＿＿＿＿＿＿ , like he was ＿＿＿＿＿ . But the food never came back down. He'd ＿＿

＿＿＿＿＿＿＿and ＿＿＿＿＿＿ .

第五步

變化招式：領悟基本動作的另一層意義

a catchy tune 容易記住，可以朗朗上口的曲調

That TV commercial had such a catchy tune that I've been humming it all day long. I can't get the song out of my head. 那個電視廣告的曲調非常好記，我一整天都在哼，想忘都忘不掉。

There's a catch. 背後隱藏著陷阱。

The movie is free, but there's a catch: you have to buy two large bags of popcorn and two large Cokes to see it without buying a ticket. 電影是免費的，但有個條件：你得買兩包大爆米花跟兩杯大可樂，才能不買票進場去看。

a catch-22 無法擺脫的困境

You can't get a job without experience, but you can't get experience without having a job—it's a catch-22. 沒經驗就找不到工作，但是沒工作又哪裡來的經驗──這真是一個無法擺脫的困局。

[17]

FINGER TIP SALAD 指尖沙拉

Injury 受傷

chapter 17 ▶

沒人喜歡受傷，但是一陣子之後你就習慣了，而且不會再感到害怕。人都免不了一死，對吧？完完整整、毫髮無傷地死去也沒啥意義，是不是？我的想法是，我要在進棺材前盡可能地衝。我打算把自己耗光。等耗完了，我也完了。

Nobody wants to get hurt. But after a while you get used to it, and you aren't afraid anymore. We're all going to die, right? There's no point in dying in perfect condition, is there? My thinking is that I want to get as much mileage out of myself as possible before I call it quits. I just plan to use myself up. When I'm done, I'm done.

現場要請到的是：[傅本基，又稱小傅，林記麵店的廚子]

I saw Ho <u>whack off</u> the end of his finger. He <u>swept it off</u> onto the floor with a pile of carrot bits before he noticed the blood. We all laughed at him. I guess we figured[1] he deserved[2] it — he was always showing off[3] with his cleaver. Tough crowd. But Ho was tougher. He <u>stabbed</u> that finger against a hot wok[4] until it started to smoke. He <u>winced</u>[5] but he never <u>cried out</u>. Then he went back to chopping carrots. That sure <u>shut us up</u>.

翻譯

　　我看到小何剁掉一節手指。他把那節指頭連同一堆紅蘿蔔丁掃到地上，之後才發現有血。大夥全都笑他，我想可能是因為覺得他活該吧——他老喜歡拿著切肉刀賣弄耍帥。冷酷的觀眾。不過小何更酷，他把那根指頭直接往熱騰騰的炒鍋上一戳，直到鍋子開始冒煙。他的臉抽搐了一下，但是他吭都沒吭一聲，之後又逕自切起紅蘿蔔來。這一幕當然讓大夥都閉上了嘴。

Word list

1. figure [ˋfɪgjɚ] v. 心想；認為
2. deserve [dɪˋzɝv] v. 應得；該受
3. show off 誇示；炫耀
4. wok [wɑk] n. 中國炒菜鍋
5. wince [wɪns] v. 退縮

CD-51

第一步

動作分解：跟唸 3-5 次紮實基本功

○ to whack off something	剁掉某物
○ to sweep something off	把某物掃掉
○ to stab	刺、戳
○ to wince	臉部肌肉抽搐；畏縮
○ to cry out	大聲叫喊
○ to shut someone up	讓某人閉嘴

CD-52

第二步

發音秘笈：跟唸 2-3 次，破除你咬字含糊、發音錯誤的弱點

自然發音： ou >> [ʌ] / [aʊ]

Tough 中 ou 的發音跟 out 中的 ou 發音不同。Tough 的發 [ʌ]，out 的則發 [aʊ]。請大聲唸出下面這些的字，練習這兩種發音：

> [練習]
> [ʌ]: enough、touch、rough
> [aʊ]: doubt、shout、loud
>
> 1. It's really cold. I **doubt** you're wearing **enough**.
>   真的很冷，我懷疑你穿的夠不夠。
> 2. If anyone **touches** you, just **shout**.
>   如果有人摸你，就大叫。

第三步

口才練功房：重新過招，學學「傅本基」的口氣、語調

I saw Ho whack off the end of his finger. He swept it off onto the floor / with a pile of carrot bits / before he noticed the blood. We all laughed at him. I guess we figured he deserved it—he was always showing off with his cleaver. Tough crowd. But Ho was tougher. He stabbed that finger against a hot wok / until it started to smoke. He winced / but he never cried out. Then he went back to chopping carrots. That sure shut us up.

換你朗讀。特別注意：

1. 基本原則請參考 [序2]

2. 如果需要多聽幾次示範，請到 CD-50 [00:06]

3. 請注意停頓、語氣的表現：

　　[/]：除了一般英文標點符號以外，可以停頓的地方。

　　[套色字]：加重語氣的字。

第四步 如果需要再聽幾次，請重播 **CD-50** [00:06]

心法修練：重播 CD，測驗自己習得幾成功力

I saw Ho _____ the end of his finger. He _____ onto the floor with a pile of carrot bits before he noticed the blood. We all laughed at him. I guess we figured he deserved it — he was always showing off with his cleaver. Tough crowd. But Ho was tougher. He _____ that finger against a hot wok until it started to smoke. He _____ but he never _____. Then he went back to chopping carrots. That sure _____.

第五步

變化招式：領悟基本動作的另一層意義

sweep into/ out of/ across/ through a place
疾速進入／離開／經過／通過某處

　　The jets swept across the sky. 噴射機劃過天際。

sweep a series (of games) 壓倒性的勝利；獲全勝

　　The New York Mets swept a seven-game series against the St. Louis Cardinals, winning the first four games in a row. 紐約大都會隊在和聖路易紅雀隊七戰四勝的比賽中，連贏前四場，大獲全勝。

sweep someone off his/her feet 令某人神魂顛倒

　　When I first met John, he swept me off my feet — I almost married him after talking to him for ten minutes. 第一次遇到約翰的時候，他就讓我神魂顛倒——和他講了十分鐘的話，就差點嫁給了他。

【18】

MAGIC HANDS
妙手春花

Massage 馬殺雞

或許我的確有一個秘密武器。她叫李章夏,是來自台灣的盲女,現在住在九龍獅子山下的一條小巷子中。每當我的狀況真的變得很糟的時候——我的意思是,只要我受了傷或很疲勞或就只是覺得非常困惑的時候——就去找她按摩。她有一雙神奇的手。我從來不跟她說我有什麼問題,但她總能找出問題。她把我裡外都摸得一清二楚——不管哪裡不對勁,她都找得出來。

Maybe I do have one secret. Her name is Li Chang-Xia. She's a blind girl from Taiwan. Now she lives on a small lane below Lion Rock in Kowloon. Whenever I really get into bad shape —I mean, whenever I'm hurt or exhausted or just real confused —I go to her for a massage. She has magic hands. I never tell her what is troubling me, but she always finds it. She knows me inside and out — whatever's wrong, she'll find it.

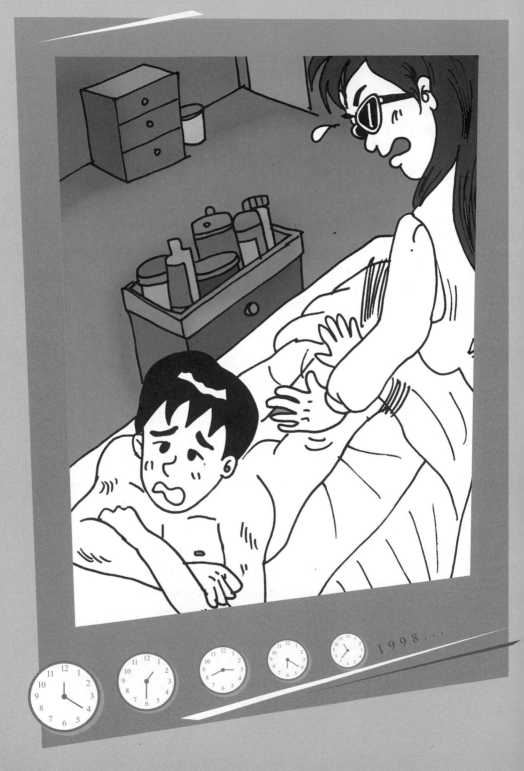

來看VCR：[李章夏，女按摩師，九龍，1998 年]

What would you do without me, Mr. Ho? These knots[1] in your back are like boulders[2]. I'll be <u>kneading</u>[3] them for hours before they're gone. I'm going to <u>spread</u> some hot oil on your shoulders first. But don't get too comfortable. I'm just <u>warming you up</u> before I really <u>dig in</u>. And I'm not going to hold back this time. <u>Take a deep breath</u>, Mr. Ho. Ready? Hey, stop <u>squirming</u>[4]—how am I supposed to fix you up when you're <u>wriggling</u>[5] <u>like a fish</u>?

翻譯

　　沒有我你怎麼辦，何先生？你背上的腫塊硬得像石頭，我要推拿好幾小時才能消除它們。我要在你的肩膀上先抹一些熱油。你可別太輕鬆自在，我這只是真正動手前幫你做的暖身，而且這次我不會有保留。深呼吸，何先生，準備好了嗎？嘿，不要扭動──你像魚一樣扭來扭去，我要怎麼搞定你這些腫塊？

Word list

1. knot [nɑt] *n.* （肌肉）硬塊；結
2. boulder [ˋboldə] *n.* 河床上的大圓石
3. knead [nid] *v.* 捏揉
4. squirm [skwɜm] *v.* 扭動身體；侷促不安
5. wriggle [ˋrɪgl] *v.* 蠕動

第一步

動作分解：跟唸 **3-5** 次紮實基本功

o **to knead** 推拿、按摩

o **to spread** 塗抹

o **to warm [somebody] up** 幫（某人）做暖身

o **to dig in** 開始認真工作

o **to take a deep breath** 深深地吸一口氣

o **to squirm** 蠕動、扭動

o **to wriggle [like a fish]** （像條魚一樣）蠕動、扭動

第二步

發音秘笈：跟唸 **2-3** 次，破除你咬字含糊、發音錯誤的弱點

　　自然發音：Kn ［n］

　　Knots 和 kneading 這兩個字的字首字母 k 均不發音。其他 k 也不發音的字還包括 know（知道）、knife （刀子）、knock （敲）、knee （膝蓋）、knuckle （手指關節）、kneel （跪）等。請練習以上提到的這些字：

[練習]

Kn [n]: knot、knead、know、knife、knock、knee、knuckle、kneel

1. If you can't untie that **kn**ot, use a **kn**ife.
   如果你解不開開那個結，就用刀子。
2. I know how to **kn**ock people down with my **kn**ee.
   我知道怎麼用膝蓋把人摔倒。

第三步

CD-53

口才練功房：重新過招，學學「李章夏」的口氣、語調

What would you do without me, Mr. Ho? These knots in your back are like boulders. I'll be kneading them for hours / before they're gone. I'm going to spread some hot oil on your shoulders first. But don't get too comfortable. I'm just warming you up / before I really dig in. And I'm not going to hold back this time. Take a deep breath, Mr. Ho. Ready? Hey, stop squirming—how am I supposed to fix you up / when you're wriggling like a fish?

換你朗讀。特別注意：

1. 基本原則請參考 [序2]
2. 如果需要多聽幾次示範，請到 CD-53 [00:06]
3. 請注意停頓、語氣的表現：
　　[/]：除了一般英文標點符號以外，可以停頓的地方。
　　[套色字]：加重語氣的字。

如果需要再聽幾次，請重播 CD-53 [00:06]

第四步

心法修練：重播 CD，測驗自己習得幾成功力

What would you do without me, Mr. Ho? These knots in your back are like boulders. I'll be _____ them for hours before they're gone. I'm going to _____ some hot oil on your shoulders first. But don't get too comfortable. I'm just _____ before I really _____. And I'm not going to hold back this time. _____, Mr. Ho. Ready? Hey, stop _____—how am I supposed to fix you up when you're _____?

第五步

變化招式：領悟基本動作的另一層意義

dig in 開動（開始吃）

　　Dinner's ready—let's dig in! I'm starving! 晚餐好了——咱們開動吧！我餓死了！

dig up some dirt on someone 挖出某人的醜行

　　The leading presidential candidate withdrew from the race because the opposing party dug up some dirt on him. 領先的總統候選人退出選戰，因為對方挖出了他的一些醜事。

dig oneself (into) a hole 自找麻煩；自掘墳墓

　　You haven't done any homework the whole semester? Wow, you've really dug yourself into a hole for the final exam. 你一整個學期都沒有做功課？哇，期末考你真是自掘墳墓。

【19】

NO CRAB WALKING !
不準學螃蟹走路！

Yoga 瑜珈

有一次我的背嚴重受創。當時我在做特技——因為耐不住性子，他們還沒把床墊放好，我就一頭從窗戶跳了出去。醫生要我做瑜珈復健。我說，好，我什麼都願意試試。但是瑜珈不適合我。我學到一些東西，例如如何正確做深呼吸。我對瑜珈沒什麼成見，但是我就是坐不住。我想做伏地挺身，惹得老師對我很不高興。

chapter 19 ▶

I hurt my back real bad once. I was doing a stunt —got impatient and jumped through a window before they'd put the mattresses down. The doctors wanted me to do yoga to get better. Fine, I said, I'll try anything. But it wasn't for me. I learned some things, like how to take a real big breath. I don't have anything bad to say about it. But I just couldn't sit still. I wanted to do push-ups. The teacher got mad at me.

1993...

來看VCR：[拉法里・艾卡恰卡拉，教練，哈薩瑜珈教室，香港，1993 年]

Mr. Ho? I'm sorry to say that one-arm push-ups are *not* part of this pose. The rest of us are sitting in Padmāsana[1]. Please <u>roll over</u> and <u>sit up</u>, Mr. Ho. <u>Cross your legs</u>. <u>Sit with your spine erect</u>[2] and <u>stretch out your arms</u>. You can <u>rest them on your knees</u> if you like. Stop <u>rolling your eyes</u> and don't <u>stick out your tongue</u>. That's Simhāsana[3], Mr. Ho! No <u>crab walking</u>! This is a pose[4] for relaxation[5]. Relax! Stop that at once, and relax!

翻譯

何先生？很抱歉，我得告訴你這個姿勢不包括單手伏地挺身。我們其他人都在做帕德瑪薩那姿勢。請翻身起來坐好，何先生。盤起腿，脊椎挺直坐著，展開雙臂。如果你喜歡，可以把手放在膝蓋上。不要再翻白眼，也不要把你的舌頭吐出來，那是西姆哈薩那姿勢。何先生！不要學螃蟹走路！這是個放鬆的姿勢。放鬆！不準再那樣了，放鬆！

Word list
1. Padmāsana [pædəmə`sanə] *n.* 蓮花坐姿
2. erect [ɪ`rɛkt] *v.* 直立
3. Simhāsana [sɪmə`sanə] *n.* 獅子坐姿
4. pose [poz] *n.* 姿勢
5. relaxation [.rilæks`eʃən] *n.* 放鬆

第一步

動作分解：跟唸 3-5 次紮實基本功

o to roll over	翻身
o to sit up	坐起來
o to cross one's legs	盤腿
o to sit with one's spine erect	脊椎挺直坐好
o to stretch out one's arms	伸展雙臂
o to rest one's arms on one's knees	雙手擺在膝蓋上
o to roll one's eyes	翻白眼
o to stick out one's tongue	吐舌頭
o to crab walk	學螃蟹走路

第二步

發音秘笈：跟唸 2-3 次，破除你咬字含糊、發音錯誤的弱點

重音和語調：

★ Push-ups are *not* part of this pose.

拉法里把重音放在 "*not*" 上的用意有二：其一是他認為比利不應該做伏地挺身，其二是他要表示對比利不高興。藉由強調 not 這個字，他表達出無法苟同比利的立場。拉法里緩慢而清楚地說出該詞，並強調最後的子音，以傳達苛責的語氣。

[練習]

1. That is *not* what I meant. 那不是我的意思。

2. If you keep up that nonsense, you are *not* going to be welcome here again. 你繼續這樣胡鬧下去，我們就不再歡迎你來了。

第三步

口才練功房：重新過招，學學「艾卡恰卡拉」的口氣、語調　CD-56

Mr. Ho? I'm sorry to say / that one-arm pushups are *not* part of this pose. The rest of us are sitting in Padmāsana. Please roll over and sit up, Mr. Ho. Cross your legs. Sit with your spine erect / and stretch out your arms. You can rest them on your knees / if you like. Stop rolling your eyes / and don't stick out your tongue. That's Simhāsana, Mr. Ho! No crab walking! This is a pose for relaxation. Relax! Stop that at once, and relax!

換你朗讀。特別注意：

1. 基本原則請參考 [序2]

2. 如果需要多聽幾次示範，請到 CD-56 [00:06]

3. 請注意停頓、語氣的表現：

　　[/]：除了一般英文標點符號以外，可以停頓的地方。

　　[套色字]：加重語氣的字。

🦶 第四步

心法修練： 重播 CD，測驗自己習得幾成功力

Mr. Ho? I'm sorry to say that one-arm push-ups are not part of this pose. The rest of us are sitting in Padmāsana. Please _____ and _____, Mr. Ho. _____. _____ and _____. You can _____ if you like. Stop _____ and don't _____. That's Simhāsana, Mr. Ho! No _____! This is a pose for relaxation. Relax! Stop that at once, and relax!

🦶 第五步

變化招式： 領悟基本動作的另一層意義

be rolling in money 非常有錢

John's not poor—in fact, he's rolling in money. 約翰不窮——事實上，他非常有錢。

roll in 大量湧進

Our new advertisements are really good—orders for our new products are rolling in so fast that we can hardly keep up. 我們新的廣告真有效——新產品的訂單不斷快速湧進，我們簡直應接不暇。

Let's roll. 動身吧。

OK, I'm ready. Let's roll, or we'll be late for the meeting. 好了，我準備好了。咱們動身吧，不然開會就要遲到了。

HOME 返鄉

Rehabilitation 復健

1983 年時，我媽生病了。我決定回家幫妹妹照顧她。我離開馬戲團，和朋友賈凡道別，然後在一艘載滿咖啡的貨船上找到一份差事。讓我長話短說：船上的自助餐廳發生爆炸起火，燒死了一些人。我則嚴重灼傷，雖然活了下來，命卻去了半條。當我回到家時，我妹妹變成有兩個人需要照顧。

In 1983, my mom got sick. I decided to go home to help my little sister take care of her. I left the circus, said goodbye to my friend Djavan, and got a job on a cargo ship loaded with coffee. To make a long story short, there was an explosion and a fire in the cafeteria. Some people got killed. I was badly burned. I survived, but just barely. When I got home, my sister had two people to look after.

chapter 20 ▶

1983...

來看VCR：[悅芳・何，比利的妹妹，九龍，1983 年]

　　Sit still, Billy! Quit <u>fidgeting</u>[1]. This is not a good time to be <u>doing leg lifts</u>, and you know it. I need to <u>clean the burns</u> on your arm and <u>wrap them with fresh bandages</u>[2]. Can you just lie there and be quiet? No? Then let me put it this way. You can and you will. If you don't, I'll <u>feed</u> your seafood porridge[3] to Mr. Tam's dog. Believe me—I'll do it. And I'll <u>bring him in</u> so you can watch him eat.

翻 譯

　　坐好，比利！不要動來動去的了，現在不是做抬腿動作的時候，你自己也很清楚。我得清理你手臂上的灼傷，並用乾淨的繃帶把它們包好。你躺好、安靜一下行不行 ？不行？那我這麼說好了。你行，而且會。如果你不照做，我就把你的海鮮粥拿去餵譚先生的狗。相信我——我說到做到。我還會把牠帶進來，讓你眼睜睜看著牠吃。

Word list | 1. fidget [ˈfɪdʒɪt] *v.* 坐立不安　　3. porridge [ˈpɔrɪdʒ] *n.* 麥片粥
2. bandage [ˈbændɪdʒ] *n.* 繃帶

第一步

動作分解：跟唸 3-5 次紮實基本功

o to fidget	坐立不安
o to do leg lifts	做抬腿動作
o to clean the burns	清理燒傷處
o to wrap the burns with bandages	用繃帶將傷口包紮起來
o to feed [something to someone]	餵（某人吃某物）
o to bring [someone] in	帶（某人）進來

第二步

發音秘笈：跟唸 2-3 次，破除你咬字含糊、發音錯誤的弱點

強音與弱音：can ≫ [kæn] / [kən]

★ **Can** you just lie there and be quiet?　[kən]

★ You **can** and you will.　[kæn]

　　一般而言，除了強調、簡答以及與否定詞 **not** 連用外，助動詞 can 唸輕音即可。試比較下列各句中 can 的唸法。

[練習]

1. **Can** you do it ?　　[kən]
2. Yes, I **can** do it.　　[kən]
3. Yes, I **can**.　　[kæn]
4. No, I **can't**.　　[kænt]

第三步 *CD-59*

口才練功房：重新過招，學學「悅芳‧何」的口氣、語調

Sit still, Billy! Quit fidgeting. This is not a good time to

be doing leg lifts, and you know it. I need to clean the burns

on your arm / and wrap them with fresh bandages. Can you

just lie there / and be quiet? No? Then let me put it this way.

You can / and you will. If you don't, I'll feed your seafood

porridge to Mr. Tam's dog. Believe me— I'll do it. And I'll

bring him in / so you can watch him eat.

換你朗讀。特別注意：
1. 基本原則請參考 [序2]
2. 如果需要多聽幾次示範，請到 CD-59 [00:06]
3. 請注意停頓、語氣的表現：
　[/]：除了一般英文標點符號以外，可以停頓的地方。
　[套色字]：加重語氣的字。

127

如果需要再聽幾次，請重播 CD-59 [00:06]

第四步

心法修練：重播CD，測驗自己習得幾成功力

Sit still, Billy! Quit _____ . This is not a good time to be _____ , and you know it. I need to _____ on your arm and _____ . Can you just lie there and be quiet? No? Then let me put it this way. You can and you will. If you don't, I'll _____ your seafood porridge to Mr. Tam's dog. Believe me — I'll do it. And I'll _____ so you can watch him eat.

第五步

變化招式：領悟基本動作的另一層意義

wrap something up 完成；收拾；善尾

Are you guys still working? Well, wrap it up. We have to go or we'll be late. 你們還在工作？好了，收拾收拾吧，再不走我們就要遲到了。

wrap one's arms around someone 緊緊擁抱某人

When the lost child finally saw his mother, he wrapped his arms around her and wouldn't let go. 當走丟的孩子總算看到母親時，他緊緊地抱住她，說什麼也不放開。

have someone wrapped around one's little finger
某人有主宰對某人的能力

Of course he'll buy the diamond ring she wants — she's got him wrapped around her little finger. 他當然會買她要的鑽石戒指送她——他對她唯命是從啊。

SECTION V

Movies
電 影

　　二十年前，比利·何躍上大銀幕，演出電影《廣州殭屍三》。在戲中他搖身一變成了可怕的殭屍頭目維瑪·張，這使得這部二流電影鹹魚翻身變成了賣座影片。從此之後，他便片約不斷，拍攝了一部又一部的賣座電影。比利，當電影明星是不是一直都是你的夢想？當你第一次得到重大突破的時候有什麼感覺？告訴我們你是如何踏入這一行的。告訴我們拍電影到底是什麼滋味。

Twenty years ago, Billy Ho burst on to the scene in *Guangzhou Zombie III*. His terrifying turn as the master zombie Vilmar Chung helped turn that B-movie into a big hit. He's been busy ever since, making hit after hit. Billy, was it always your dream to become a movie star? How'd you feel when you got your first big break? Tell us how you got started in the business. Tell us what it's really like to work in the movies.

【21】
GUANGZHOU ZOMBIE III
《廣州殭屍三》
Makeup 化妝

　　我從來沒有計畫要成為電影明星，只是機運好罷了。在我的灼傷痊癒，我媽也逐漸康復之後，我去找以前的老闆劉先生。我問他是不是仍然很氣他那隻蟋蟀的事，他聽了大笑，說他現在在製作電影。他說拍電影比鬥蟋蟀更賺錢。好賺太多了。他問我想不想在電影裡軋一角，我說：「當然好，有何不可？」

　　I never planned to become a movie star. I just lucked into it. After I recovered from the burns, and after my mom was doing better, I went to see my old boss, Mr. Lau. I asked him if he was still mad about his cricket. He laughed and said he was producing movies now. He said there was more money in movies than in crickets. Lots more. He asked me if I'd like to be in a movie. I said, "Sure, why not?"

CD-62

來看VCR：[薇若妮卡·宋，化妝師，《廣州殭屍三》拍片現場，1983 年]

Whoa! Your arm already looks like a zombie[1] arm! Uh, I meant that as a compliment[2]. Sorry — that was a stupid thing to say. But those really *are* some impressive[3] scars! I won't have to <u>apply any makeup</u> at all — I might just <u>daub[4] on</u> some fake blood, maybe <u>touch up</u> the scars to make them look like fresh wounds. I'll <u>pencil</u> your eyelids red and <u>brush on</u> some white powder to make your face look dead. Don't worry. You're gonna be a *great* zombie.

翻 譯

　　哇賽！你的手臂看起來像殭屍手臂了！呃，我這是稱讚的意思。對不起——我說的是蠢話。不過你這些疤**的確**真夠嚇人！我根本不需要再上什麼妝——可能只要在上面抹一點假血，或者補一點妝，讓它看起來像新鮮的傷口就行了。我會把你的眼皮畫成紅色的，然後在你臉上刷一些白粉，讓你臉看起來像死人。別擔心，你會是**一級棒**的殭屍。

Word list
1. zombie [ˋzɔmbɪ] *n.* 還魂復活的屍體
2. compliment [ˋkɑmpləmənt] *n.* 讚美
3. impressive [ɪmˋprɛsɪv] *adj.* 令人難忘的
4. daub [dɔb] *v.* 塗

第一步

動作分解：跟唸 3-5 次紮實基本功

o to apply makeup	上妝
o to daub on	塗抹上
o to touch up	做點修補
o to pencil	用筆畫
o to brush on	用刷子刷上

第二步

發音秘笈：跟唸 2-3 次，破除你咬字含糊、發音錯誤的弱點

減化音：going to >> gonna [`gʌnə]

★ You're **gonna** be a *great* zombie.

美國人經常會把 "going to" 說成 "gonna" [`gʌnə]。請注意聽薇若妮卡是怎麼說上面這句話的。

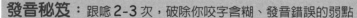

[練習]

1. I'm **gonna** do some study tonight. 今晚我要讀點書。

2. She's **gonna** marry him next month. 她下個月要嫁給他。

第三步

CD-62

口才練功房：重新過招，學學「薇若妮卡·宋」的口氣、語調

Whoa! Your arm already looks like a zombie arm! Uh, I

meant that as a compliment. Sorry — that was a stupid thing

to say. But those really *are* some impressive scars! I won't

have to apply any makeup at all — I might just daub on some

fake blood, maybe touch up the scars / to make them look like

fresh wounds. I'll pencil your eyelids red / and brush on some

white powder / to make your face look dead. Don't worry.

You're gonna be a *great* zombie.

換你朗讀。特別注意：
1. 基本原則請參考 [序2]
2. 如果需要多聽幾次示範，請到 CD-62 [00:22]
3. 請注意停頓、語氣的表現：
　　[/]：除了一般英文標點符號以外，可以停頓的地方。
　　[套色字]：加重語氣的字。

如果需要再聽幾次，請重播 **CD-62** [00:22]

第四步

心法修練：重播CD，測驗自己習得幾成功力

Whoa! Your arm already looks like a zombie arm! Uh, I meant that as a compliment. Sorry—that was a stupid thing to say. But those really are some impressive scars! I won't have to _____ at all—I might just _____ some fake blood, maybe _____ the scars to make them look like fresh wounds. I'll _____ your eyelids red and _____ some white powder to make your face look dead. Don't worry. You're gonna be a great zombie.

第五步

變化招式：領悟基本動作的另一層意義

brush something 輕輕擦過某物

Luckily, he didn't crash his motorcycle directly into the wall. He just brushed it. 幸虧他沒有騎著摩托車直接撞上牆壁。他只是輕微擦撞到。

brush up on something 溫習某物

Billy brushed up on his lines immediately before filming each of his scenes. 在快開拍每一個鏡頭之前，比利都會溫習他的台詞。

brush someone off 不理會某人

Josey's such a snob. When I said hello to her at the party, she just brushed me off. 喬希真是個自命不凡的人。在派對中，我跟她打招呼，她居然不理會我。

[22]

ZOMBIE FUN
扮殭屍樂無窮
Stunts 特技演出

其實我是半殭屍、半人——我不必像其他的殭屍演員，必須放慢動作、裝出死人的樣子。我可以快速的移動。導演覺得我看起來挺邪惡的，於是把我晉升為殭屍頭子，讓我追著電影的主角和他的女朋友跑。我也可以咬那女的腳踝。我很喜歡搞特技，也有一些改變的好點子。我即興要了一些特技。當殭屍真好玩。

Actually, I was half-zombie, half-man — I didn't have to act slow and dead like the other zombies. I could still move fast. The directors thought I looked pretty evil so they promoted me to head zombie and I got to chase after the star of the movie and his girl. I got to bite her ankle. I enjoyed the stunt work. I had some good ideas for improvements, too. I improvised a few things. Being a zombie was fun.

chapter 22 ▶

現場邀請到的是：[艾倫·湯—卡夫曼，助理導演，《廣州殭屍三》]

I told Ho to take three steps and <u>dive</u> through the window. Somehow, he <u>missed</u>. His head <u>crashed</u> right through the wall. My heart stopped. He started to <u>snarl</u>[1] and <u>gnash</u>[2] <u>his teeth</u>. Then he <u>punched</u> a hand through the wall and <u>clawed at</u> our hero. Poor guy just about <u>peed his pants</u>. I mean, *I* was behind the camera, and *I* was scared. I thought for a second Ho was truly rabid[3] or something. It was brilliant[4]. Truly terrifying[5]. Best scene in the movie.

翻譯

　　我叫小何說跑三步然後從窗戶跳出去，哪知道他衝偏了，一頭撞穿了牆壁。我的心臟都停了。他開始咆哮，咬牙切齒，然後一拳打穿牆壁，用手抓我們的男主角。可憐的傢伙差一點就尿褲子。我是說，我在攝影機後面，連我都嚇得要死。有那麼片刻鐘我還想小何是不是真的得了狂犬病之類的。這一幕棒透了，恐怖至極，是這部電影中最棒的一幕。

Word list

1. snarl [snɑrl] *v.* 咆哮
2. gnash [næʃ] *v.* 咬牙切齒
3. rabid [ˋræbɪd] *adj.* 狂暴的；患狂犬病的
4. brilliant [ˋbrɪlɪənt] *adj.* 精彩的；卓越的
5. terrifying [ˋtɛrɪfaɪɪŋ] *adj.* 駭人的

第一步

動作分解：跟唸 3-5 次紮實基本功

o to dive	俯衝而下
o to miss	未中目標
o to crash [through a wall]	撞（穿牆壁）
o to snarl	咆哮
o to gnash one's teeth	咬牙；磨牙
o to punch [through a wall]	一拳打（穿牆壁）
o to claw at [someone]	抓（某人）
o to pee one's pants	尿褲子

第二步

發音秘笈：跟唸 2-3 次，破除你咬字含糊、發音錯誤的弱點

連音： just about >> justabout [`jʌstəbaʊt]

★ Poor guy **just about** peed his pants.

　　說話要聽起來像英語人士，有時候得注意如何把句子中的字詞串連起來，不能只注重每個字的個別發音。以 "Just about" 這個常見的片語為例，請聽湯瑪士如何將 just 最後面的字音 [t] 和 about 前面的母音 [ə] 連起來。

[練習]

Don't tell anyone, but it's true — I **just about** peed my pants. Then, I **just about** fainted. 別跟任何人說，不過是真的——我差一點尿褲子，之後又差一點昏倒。

口才練功房：重新過招，學學「艾倫‧湯」的口氣、語調

I told Ho to take three steps / and dive through the window. Somehow, he missed. His head crashed right through the wall. My heart stopped. He started to snarl / and gnash his teeth. Then he punched a hand through the wall / and clawed at our hero. Poor guy just about peed his pants. I mean, I was behind the camera, and *I* was scared. I thought for a second Ho was truly rabid or something. It was brilliant. Truly terrifying. Best scene in the movie.

換你朗讀。特別注意：
1. 基本原則請參考 [序2]
2. 如果需要多聽幾次示範，請到 CD-65 [00:05]
3. 請注意停頓、語氣的表現：
　　[/]：除了一般英文標點符號以外，可以停頓的地方。
　　[套色字]：加重語氣的字。

如果需要再聽幾次，請重播 CD-65 [00:05]

心法修練： 重播CD，測驗自己習得幾成功力

I told Ho to take three steps and _____ through the window. Somehow, he _____ . His head _____ right through the wall. My heart stopped. He started to _____ and _____ . Then he _____ a hand through the wall and _____ our hero. Poor guy just about _____ . I mean, I was behind the camera, and I was scared. I thought for a second Ho was truly rabid or something. It was brilliant. Truly terrifying. Best scene in the movie.

第五步

變化招式： 領悟基本動作的另一層意義

take a dive/nosedive 暴跌；急降；突然變壞

Stock prices took a nosedive today, and were down twenty percent on average when the market closed. 今天股價暴跌，股市收盤時，平均下跌二成。

a dive 低級酒館；低級夜總會

I don't want to go to Mel's Pub again. That place is a dive! 我再也不想上梅爾酒館了。那地方爛透了。

dumpster-diving 翻垃圾桶（找重要資料）

You'd better check your credit card statements for unauthorized purchases; the police caught some guys dumpster-diving in our trash last night. 你最好檢查一下信用卡帳單的明細表，看有沒有被盜刷。昨晚警察逮到幾個傢伙在翻我們的垃圾桶。

[23]

ADRIAN YIP
艾迪恩・葉

Putting Up with a Movie Star 對電影明星忍氣吞聲

並不是天天有人付錢給你演殭屍的。我每天醒來都感覺自己很幸運，心裡在想：今天我可以演殭屍。唯一的問題是大明星主角葉先生。他真是個大豬頭，把每個人都當成下人。他老在想讓人知道他是主角，就連攝影機停機的時候也一樣。我都忍了下來——盡可能地忍——因為我不想丟掉工作。

chapter 23 ▶

It isn't every day that somebody pays you to be a zombie. Every day I woke up and felt lucky, thinking: I get to be a zombie today. The only problem was the star, Mr. Yip. He had a big fat head, treated everybody like a servant. He was always trying to let you know that he was the star, even when the cameras weren't running. I put up with it — for as long as I could — because I didn't want to lose my job.

來看 VCR：[艾迪恩‧葉，電影明星，《廣州殭屍三》的拍片現場，1983 年]

Ho? Last time I checked, that was my chair. Yep, there's my name, written right on it—can't you read? Ugh—that zombie gunk is <u>flaking[1] off your face</u>. Get up. <u>Brush that mess off my chair</u>. And while you're at it, <u>pour</u> me some tea. Oh—and, Ho? <u>Settle down</u> on the set[2], would you? We've all had about enough of your amateur[3] improvisations[4]. Don't <u>glare</u> at me, Ho. Please. <u>Back off</u> and learn your place—or I'll have you <u>sacked</u>[5]. Now <u>get lost</u>.

翻譯

　　小何？就我所知，那是我的椅子。沒錯，有我的名字，上面寫得一清二楚——你不識字呀？嗯——你臉上塗的殭屍白糊已經開始在脫妝剝落了。站起來，把我椅子上的髒東西拂掉，也順便幫我倒一杯茶來。哦，還有——小何？在片場時安分一點，可以嗎？我們都受夠你那些不入流的即興表演了。不要瞪著我，小何。拜託，退後，識相點——不然我就把你換掉。好了，滾吧。

Word list
1. flake [flɛk] v. 成薄片剝落
2. be on the set 在內景
3. amateur [ˈæmə.tʃʊə] adj. 業餘的
4. improvisation [ˌɪmprəvaɪˈzeʃən] n. 即興創作
5. sack [sæk] v. 解雇

第一步

動作分解：跟唸 3-5 次紮實基本功

o to flake off [one's face]	（從某人臉上）剝落下來
o to brush [something] off [somewhere]	拂去（某處上的某物）
o to pour [someone some tea]	倒（茶給某人）
o to settle down	安分下來
o to glare at [someone]	怒目而視（某人）
o to back off	退後
o to sack someone	辭退某人
o Get lost!	滾開！

第二步

發音秘笈：跟唸 2-3 次，破除你咬字含糊、發音錯誤的弱點

困難發音：短母音 [ɛ] vs. 長母音 [e]

英文中最常混淆的兩個音就是短音 [ɛ]（如 mess）和長音 [e]（如 name）。再聽一次艾迪恩・葉說過的幾句話，看你能否分辨出這兩個音，並試著把這些句子唸出來。

[練習]
短母音 [ɛ]：check、chair、mess、set、glare
長母音 [e]：name、flake、face、place

1. Last time I **checked**, that was my **chair**.
2. There's my **name**.

第三步

口才練功房：重新過招，學學「艾迪恩‧葉」的口氣、語調

Ho? Last time I checked, that was my chair. Yep, there's my name, written right on it—can't you read? Ugh—that zombie gunk / is flaking off your face. Get up. Brush that mess / off my chair. And while you're at it, pour me some tea. Oh—and, Ho? Settle down on the set, would you? We've all had about enough of your amateur improvisations. Don't glare at me, Ho. Please. Back off / and learn your place—or I'll have you sacked. Now get lost.

換你朗讀。特別注意：

1. 基本原則請參考 [序2]

2. 如果需要多聽幾次示範，請到 CD-68 [00:07]

3. 請注意停頓、語氣的表現：

　　[/]：除了一般英文標點符號以外，可以停頓的地方。

　　[⌒]：特殊音調上揚或下降。

　　[套色字]：加重語氣的字。

如果需要再聽幾次，請重播 CD-68 [00:07]

第四步

心法修練： 重播 CD，測驗自己習得幾成功力

Ho? Last time I checked, that was my chair. Yep, there's my name, written right on it — can't you read? Ugh — that zombie gunk is _____ . Get up. _____ . And while you're at it, _____ me some tea. Oh — and, Ho? _____ on the set, would you? We've all had about enough of your amateur improvisations. Don't _____ at me, Ho. Please. _____ and learn your place — or I'll have you _____ . Now _____ .

第五步

變化招式： 領悟基本動作的另一層意義

a flake 怪人

I don't want to go to lunch with Denny — he's such a flake. 我不想和丹尼去吃午餐——他是個怪腳。

flake out 抓狂；失控

When we asked the boss a question at the meeting, he just flaked out and started yelling at everybody. 開會時我們問老闆一個問題，結果他突然失控，開始對著每個人大吼大叫。

flaky/flakey 古里古怪的；層層疊疊的

Tammy is a flaky person, but a great pastry chef. Her pies have a delicious, flaky crust. 譚美是個古怪的人，但卻是一級棒的糕點廚師。她做的派有一層層好吃的派皮。

【24】

SCARING YIP
嚇老葉
Scare the Shit Out of the Star
大明星嚇破膽

　　剛開始的時候，又是攝影機、又是導演、又是名人的，我有點畏懼。我意思是，對我而言那真的是個不同的世界。你很難想像我媽和我妹看到我演電影，有多興奮。於是我就努力去適應，並沒有製造任何麻煩。我努力當好一個殭屍，也盡量不理會姓葉的。但是一個人的忍耐是有限度的。

　　At first, I was a little bit awed by the cameras and the directors and the famous people. I mean, it was really a different life for me. You can't imagine how excited my mom and my sister were to see me in a movie. So I just tried to fit in, and I didn't start any trouble. I tried to be a good zombie. I tried to ignore Yip. But everybody has his limit.

現場邀請到的是：[艾倫‧湯──考夫曼，助理導演，《廣州殭屍三》]

Final battle. Construction[1] site. Yip is supposed to <u>slay</u> Ho, supposed to <u>skewer</u>[2] him with a forklift[3]. But it doesn't go that way. Ho goes rabid again. He <u>gets a hold of</u> Yip's neck, <u>pins</u> him against a wall, <u>whispers</u> something into his ear. Yip starts <u>screaming</u>—screaming like a real zombie is about to <u>tear his throat out</u>. A girl—one of the extras[4], I think— <u>freaks out</u>, grabs a board, and <u>swings</u> at Ho. Ho <u>whips around</u>, <u>smashes</u> the board into smithereens[5], and <u>kicks her feet out from under her</u>. Never lets go of Yip's neck with the other hand. I tell you, it was scary.

翻譯

　　最後大戰。工地。原本老葉應該要殺死小何，應該用叉式堆高機戳穿他的，但是實際拍攝時卻不是那麼一回事。小何再度抓狂。他一把抓住老葉的脖子，把他按在牆上，然後在他耳邊小聲說了幾句話。老葉開始尖叫──聽起來就好像真有殭屍要撕爛他的喉嚨似的。有個女孩──我想是臨時演員之一──嚇得整個人失控，抓了一個板子就往小何身上揮過去。小何猛然轉身，把板子擊成碎片，然後踢她的腳把她絆倒在地上，另一手仍牢牢抓住老葉的脖子。我跟你說，真是嚇死人了。

Word list

1. construction [kən`strʌkʃən] *n.* 建築；施工
2. skewer [`skjuə] *v.* 叉；串
3. forklift [`fɔrk͵lɪft] *n.* 堆高機
4. extra [`ɛkstrə] *n.* 臨時雇員
5. smithereens [͵smɪθə`rinz] *n.* 碎片

151

第一步

動作分解：跟唸 3-5 次紮實基本功

o **to slay** 殘殺 　　　　o **to skewer** 叉刺

o **to get a hold of [something]** 抓住（某物）

o **to pin [somebody against a wall]** 把某人按在牆壁

o **to whisper [something into someone's ear]**
（在某人耳邊）低聲說（某事）

o **to scream** 尖叫 　　o **to tear [something] out** 撕裂（某物）

o **to freak [out]** 抓狂

o **to swing [something]** 揮動（某物）

o **to whip around** 突然轉身

o **to smash [something into smithereens]** 把某物擊破成碎片

o **to kick someone's feet out from under him/her**
踢某人的腳將他／她絆倒在地

第二步

發音秘笈：跟唸 2-3 次，破除你咬字含糊、發音錯誤的弱點

發音：連續多個子音

　　一個字當中如連續出現多個子音，有時會對某些人造成很大的困擾。比如，有人會在子音與子音之間加上一個母音：[ə]。這是萬萬不可的，一定要加以避免。熟能生巧，最好的方法當然是多練習。

[練習]
多個子音：construction、forklift、whispers、extras
I saw a **forklift** on the **construction** site. 我在工地看到一部堆高機。

第三步

口才練功房：重新過招，學學「艾倫‧湯」的口氣、語調

CD-71

Final battle. Construction site. Yip is supposed to slay Ho, supposed to skewer him with a forklift. But it doesn't go that way. Ho goes rabid again. He gets a hold of Yip's neck, pins him against a wall, whispers something into his ear. Yip starts screaming—screaming like a real zombie is about to tear his throat out. A girl— one of the extras, I think — freaks out, grabs a board, and swings at Ho. Ho whips around, smashes the board into smithereens, and kicks her feet out from under her. Never lets go of Yip's neck with the other hand. I tell you, it was scary.

換你朗讀。特別注意：

1. 基本原則請參考 [序2]

2. 如果需要多聽幾次示範，請到 CD-71 [00:07]

3. 請注意停頓、語氣的表現：

　　[/]：除了一般英文標點符號以外，可以停頓的地方。

　　[套色字]：加重語氣的字。

如果需要再聽幾次，請重播 **CD-71** [00:07]

第四步

心法修練：重播 CD，測驗自己習得幾成功力

Final battle. Construction site. Yip is supposed to _____ Ho, supposed to _____ him with a forklift. But it doesn't go that way. Ho goes rabid again. He _____ Yip's neck, _____ him against a wall, _____ something into his ear. Yip starts _____ — screaming like a real zombie is about to _____. A girl-one of the extras, I think — _____, grabs a board, and _____ at Ho. Ho _____, _____ the board into smithereens, and _____. Never lets go of Yip's neck with the other hand. I tell you, it was scary.

第五步

變化招式：領悟基本動作的另一層意義

whip 快速丟出

When the runner tried to steal, the catcher whipped the ball to second base. 跑者試圖盜壘時，捕手快速將球投到二壘。

whip out something 猛然拿出、拔出某物

The bank robber whipped out a gun and threatened everyone in the bank. 銀行搶匪猛然掏出一把槍，威脅銀行裡面所有的人。

whip somebody 將某人打得落花流水

I'm so embarrassed — our baseball team was whipped by a group of young kids. They really whipped us. 我覺得好丟臉——我們的棒球隊被一群小鬼打得落花流水。他們真的徹底擊敗了我們。

【25】

STAR 主角
Accepting Stardom
進入演藝圈

那一次事件後，老葉就試圖鼓動大家抵制這部電影。接著又打起官司。劉先生把事情解決了。事實上，他是派了來福和火腿頭山米來處理的。最後他們保留了我的戲份，我也保住了飯碗。事實上，我還被升了級。他們踢出老葉，改請我當《廣州殭屍四》的主角。老實說，不能繼續當殭屍，剛開始我還真有一點難過。

After the incident, Yip tried to organize a boycott of the movie. And there was a lawsuit. Mr. Lau handled it. Actually, he sent Lucky and Ham Head Sammy to take care of it. In the end they kept my scenes and I kept my job. Actually, I got promoted. They got rid of Yip and they asked me to be the star of *Guangzhou Zombie IV*. To be honest, I was a little sorry at first that I wouldn't get to be a zombie again.

1 9 8 3 · · ·

來看VCR：[劉先生，製作人，劉氏製片公司，九龍，1983 年]

It's really up to you, Billy. But there are some distinct[1] advantages[2] to being the star rather than a zombie. First of all, the star gets a lot more money. Also, you get to <u>smooch[3] with</u> the leading lady, rather than <u>gnaw[4] on</u> her detached[5] leg like last time. And we'll let you do that stunt you wanted—what was it? I forget... <u>slide down</u> a burning ladder while you <u>fire your pistols[6]</u>? What do you say? Deal? Good. <u>Sign</u> right here. You're a star now, Billy.

翻譯

　　一切由你決定，比利。不過比起當殭屍，當主角有一些明顯的好處。首先，主角拿的錢多得多。此外，你還可以擁抱親吻女主角，不必像上次一樣只能啃她的斷腿。而且我們也會讓你做你想做的特技——那是什麼動作來著？我忘了……一邊溜下著火的梯子，一邊開槍？怎麼樣？接受了？很好，在這裡簽名。現在你是大明星了，比利。

Word list

1. distinct [dɪˋtɪŋkt] *adj.* 清楚明白的
2. advantage [ədˋvæntɪdʒ] *n.* 好處
3. smooch [smutʃ] *v.* 擁吻
4. gnaw [nɔ] *v.* 啃咬
5. detached [dɪˋtætʃt] *adj.* 脫離的
6. pistol [ˋpɪstl] *n.* 手槍

第一步

動作分解：跟唸 3-5 次紮實基本功

o to smooch with [someone]	擁抱親吻（某人）
o to gnaw on [something]	啃咬（某物）
o to slide down [something]	（從某物上）滑下
o to fire a pistol	開槍
o to sign	簽名

第二步

發音秘笈：跟唸 2-3 次，破除你咬字含糊、發音錯誤的弱點

減化音：What do you...? >> Whadaya...? [ˋhwɑdəjə]
★ **What do you** say? Deal?

英語人士講話時，不一定會把每一個字都清清楚楚地說出來。如次 "What do you...?" 起首的句子，他們習慣將這些字詞連在一起，使用減化音來唸，聽起來就像：Whadaya...? [ˋhwɑdəjə]

[練習]

1. The right decision is to accept the deal. **Whadaya** say?
   正確的決定是接受這個交易。你認為怎麼樣？

2. **Whatadaya** say, let's slay some zombies!
   怎麼樣？讓我們殺他幾個殭屍吧！

第三步

口才練功房：重新過招，學學「劉先生」的口氣、語調

It's really up to you, Billy. But there are some distinct

advantages / to being the star rather than a zombie. First of

all, the star gets a lot more money. Also, you get to smooch

with the leading lady, rather than gnaw on her detached leg /

like last time. And we'll let you do that stunt you wanted —

what was it? I forget... slide down a burning ladder / while

you fire your pistols? Whadaya say? Deal? Good. Sign right

here. You're a star now, Billy.

換你朗讀。特別注意：

1. 基本原則請參考 [序2]

2. 如果需要多聽幾次示範，請到 CD-74 [00:06]

3. 請注意停頓、語氣的表現：

   [/]：除了一般英文標點符號以外，可以停頓的地方。

   [套色字]：加重語氣的字。

如果需要再聽幾次，請重播 CD-74 [00:06]

第四步

心法修練：重播 CD，測驗自己習得幾成功力

It's really up to you, Billy. But there are some distinct advantages to being the star rather than a zombie. First of all, the star gets a lot more money. Also, you get to _____ the leading lady, rather than _____ her detached leg like last time. And we'll let you do that stunt you wanted — what was it? I forget... _____ a burning ladder while you _____? What do you say? Deal? Good. _____ right here. You're a star now, Billy.

第五步

變化招式：領悟基本動作的另一層意義

gnaw at someone 煩惱、折磨某人

The problem gnawed at the engineer until he solved it. 那個問題深深困擾工程師，直到他解決為止。

gnawing hunger/cold/poverty 折磨人的飢餓、寒冷、窮困

The poor inhabitants of the mountain village faced gnawing cold in the winter and gnawing poverty all year long. 山上村落可憐的居民要忍受刺骨的寒冬，又要忍受一整年的窮苦。

gnaw away 逐漸消耗、侵蝕

The rushing water gnawed away the riverbank. 奔騰的河水侵蝕了河岸。

Action and Adventure

行動與冒險

　　比利，每次在看過你拍的電影之後，我都常覺得需要吃鎮定劑。《你死定了、你完蛋了》那部片子中的一些特技看得我幾乎要心臟病發。我好奇的是：就算在工作以外的時間，你好像也很好動、愛冒險。有拍片空檔的時候，你就去爬山、到叢林裡划獨木舟。聽說你以前甚至會利用拍片空檔，從事高危險性的工作，純粹只為了好玩而已。是真的嗎？寧願不坐在游泳池旁輕鬆一下？你從來不考慮安全嗎？

　　Billy, after watching one of your movies, I often feel like I need a tranquilizer. Some of the stunts in *You're Dead, You're Done* just about put me into cardiac arrest. What I'm curious about is this: even when you're not working, you still seem to have an appetite for action and adventure. In between movies, you climb mountains and paddle canoes around in jungles. I've heard that you even used to take dangerous jobs between movies, just for the fun of it. Is that true? Wouldn't rather just sit by the pool and relax? Don't you ever play it safe?

[26]

PARTY IN BAHIA
巴伊亞的狂歡派對
Blowing All Your Money
揮霍金錢

我喜歡拍電影，但是來真的比只是假裝好玩。拍電影的時候，有時我會做白日夢，想像自己在叢林探險或爬山或做其他事情。但是在做這些事情的時候，我從來不會想到：「真希望現在我在拍片現場。」拿到《廣州殭屍四》的片酬之後，我把一半的薪水給了我媽，然後帶著另一半的錢回到了巴西。

I like making movies. But it's more fun to do stuff for real rather than just to pretend to do stuff. When I'm making a movie, sometimes I daydream about being in the jungle or going to the mountains or doing some other thing. But when I'm doing those other things, I never find myself thinking, "I wish I were on a movie set." After I got paid for *Zombie IV*, I gave half the money to my mother. With the other half I went back to Brazil.

chapter 26

現場邀請到的是：[賈凡・迪奧達多]

Billy found me drinking at Lua's in Salvador. He had more money than I'd ever seen in my entire life—all <u>stuffed</u> into a plastic[1] bag. He <u>yanked</u>[2] a handful out and <u>slammed</u> it down on the bar and said, "Djavan, let's <u>throw a party</u>." I said, "Billy, you don't want to blow all that." But he was already <u>knocking back a drink</u>. The bar girls were <u>circling</u> like sharks, <u>eyeing</u> the cash. Another drunk guy at the bar threw up his hands and yelled, "That's the spirit[3]! Let's go for it!" There was no turning back.

翻譯

比利找到我的時候我正在薩爾瓦多的路雅酒館裡喝酒。他身上的錢比我一輩子看過的還多——全塞在一只塑膠袋中。他抽出一大把鈔票，砰地一聲放在吧檯上，說：「賈凡，我們開個派對吧。」我說：「比利，你可別把錢都花光了。」但是他已經仰頭乾了一杯酒。酒吧裡面的女孩子全部像鯊魚一樣圍著他打轉，眼睛盯著現金看。酒吧裡另外一個醉醺醺的傢伙高舉雙手，大喊：「這才像話！咱們開派對吧！」自此再也無法回頭。

Word list　　1. plastic [ˋplæstɪk] *adj.* 塑膠的　　3. spirit [ˋspɪrɪt] *n.* 精神；氣勢
　　　　　　　　2. yank [jæŋk] *v.* 猛拉

CD-78

第一步

動作分解：跟唸3-5次紮實基本功

o to stuff	塞
o to yank [something out]	使勁將某物拉出
o to slam [something down]	砰一聲放下某物；使勁摔某物
o to throw a party	開派對
o to knock back a drink	大口喝掉
o to circle [like a shark]	（像鯊魚一樣）繞著打轉
o to eye [something]	盯著（某物）看

第二步

CD-79

發音秘笈：跟唸2-3次，破除你咬字含糊、發音錯誤的弱點

發音：字尾 -ed >> [t] / [d]

動詞後面加 -ed，形成簡單過去式時，-ed 有兩種發音。以 [p]、[k]、[f]、[s]、[tʃ] 等無聲子音結尾的動詞接上 -ed 時，-ed 發 [t] 音；以有聲子音結尾的動詞，後面接的 -ed 則發 [d] 音。另外要特別注意，如果原來字尾已經是 -t 或 -d 的動詞，再加上過去式字尾 -ed 的時候，-ed要發 [ɪd]。

[練習]

1. He knock**ed** back a drink. 他仰頭乾了一杯酒。

2. When the pile start**ed** looking small, he reach**ed** into his plastic bag for more cash. 在那一疊鈔票看起來快用完的時候，他把手伸進塑膠袋內，掏出更多的現金。

第三步　

口才練功房：重新過招，學學「迪奧達多」的口氣、語調

Billy found me drinking at Lua's in Salvador. He had more

money / than I'd ever seen in my entire life — all stuffed into

a plastic bag. He yanked a handful out / and slammed it down

on the bar / and said, "Djavan, let's throw a party." I said,

"Billy, you don't want to blow all that." But he was already

knocking back a drink. The bar girls were circling like sharks,

eyeing the cash. Another drunk guy at the bar threw up his

hands / and yelled, "That's the spirit! Let's go for it!" There

was no turning back.

換你朗讀。特別注意：

1. 基本原則請參考 [序2]

2. 如果需要多聽幾次示範，請到 CD-77 [00:23]

3. 請注意停頓、語氣的表現：

　　[/]：除了一般英文標點符號以外，可以停頓的地方。

　　[套色字]：加重語氣的字。

心法修練：重播CD，測驗自己習得幾成功力

　　Billy found me drinking at Lua's in Salvador. He had more money than I'd ever seen in my entire life — all _____ into a plastic bag. He _____ a handful out and _____ it down on the bar and said, "Djavan, let's _____ ." I said, "Billy, you don't want to blow all that." But he was already _____ . The bar girls were _____ like sharks, _____ the cash. Another drunk guy at the bar threw up his hands and yelled, "That's the spirit! Let's go for it!" There was no turning back.

第五步

變化招式：領悟基本動作的另一層意義

throw a game/fight 故意輸掉比賽

　　Even Jake Lamotta, one of the most competitive boxers in the history of the sport, once threw a fight. 連杰克‧拉莫塔，拳擊運動史上最強的拳手之一，都曾經故意輸掉比賽。

throw in the towel 投降；放棄

　　The computer programmer couldn't figure out how to solve the problem, so he threw in the towel and went home. 該電腦工程師找不出解決問題的辦法，於是乾脆放棄回家了。

a throwback 返祖；復古

　　Nobody paints so realistically anymore. This artist really is a throwback to the Dutch masters. 現在已經沒有人畫這麼寫實的畫了。這個畫家倒真是回歸荷蘭大師的畫風。

[27]

HIGH RISE HUMOR
高樓上的幽默
Acrobatics 高空雜技

　　每拍玩一兩部電影，我就會回到巴西。有時候我會找一份差事做。我不需要那些錢，只是懷念那些工作，而且在香港我不可能找到正常的差事——我太有名了，但是在巴西根本沒有人認識我。我做自己熟悉的工作；我當廚子、在貝林的港口當碼頭工。我也在聖保羅幫忙蓋摩天大樓——我在《你死定了、你完蛋了》中演出的特技，靈感就是在那個時候想到的。

chapter 27 ▶

　　After every movie or two, I'd go back to Brazil. Sometimes I'd take a job. I didn't need the money. I just missed the work, and it would've been impossible for me to take a normal job in Hong Kong — I was too famous. But nobody knew me in Brazil. I worked at stuff I knew. I cooked, worked the docks in Belem. I helped put up a skyscraper in Sao Paolo — that's where I got the idea for that stunt I did in *You're Dead, You're Done.*

現場邀請的是：[何里歐‧瑟夫里諾，工頭，巴西聖保羅]

Billy was nuts. Once he walked out to the end of a beam[1] on the 38th floor. He <u>stood at attention</u>[2] facing out at the sky and <u>put his hands together like he was praying</u>. Then he turned around, <u>waved goodbye</u>, and <u>stepped off</u>. We <u>ran over</u> expecting[3] to see him <u>splattered</u>[4] all over the ground. But he was <u>hanging by one hand</u> from the underside of the beam, laughing. When he saw our scared faces, he laughed so hard he almost <u>lost his grip</u> and <u>slipped off</u>.

翻譯

　　比利是個瘋子。有一次他在三十八樓走到鋼樑末端，立正站好，面對著天空，雙手握在一起，像是在禱告。然後轉過身來，揮揮手說再見，接著就跨了出去。大夥兒衝過去，以為會看到他摔在，地上血肉模糊。誰知道他卻一手抓著鋼樑下方吊在那兒，縱聲大笑。當他看到我們的臉部都嚇白了，他笑得更得意，還差一點失手掉下去。

Word list | 1. beam [bim] n. 鋼樑；方木 | 3. expect [ɪksˋpɛkt] v. 期待
| 2. attention [əˋtɛnʃən] n. 注意力 | 4. splatter [ˋsplætə] v. 潑濺

第一步

動作分解：跟唸 **3-5** 次紮實基本功

o **to stand at attention**	立正站好
o **to put one's hands together [like one is praying]** 雙手握在一起（像是在禱告）	
o **to wave goodbye**	揮手說再見
o **to step off [something]** 跨出（某物） o **to run over** 跑過去	
o **to splatter [all over the ground]**	濺灑（滿地）
o **to hang by one hand**	單手抓住某物懸吊著
o **to lose one's grip** 失手 o **to slip off** 鬆拖往下掉	

第二步

發音秘笈：跟唸 **2-3** 次，破除你咬字含糊、發音錯誤的弱點

減化音：his ≫ 'is

★ He **put'is** hands together **lik'e** was praying... He laughed so hard he almost **lost'is** grip.

口語英文當中，he、him、his、her 和 hers 等代名詞經常都會被減化。英語人士經常省略這些字字首的 [h] 子音，然後用前面一個字的字尾子音把這個字的母音連接起來。

[練習]

1. They said**'is** sense of humor was quite odd.
   他們說他的幽默感相當怪異怪。

2. I thought we'd see**'im** in pieces on the ground.
   我以為我們會看到他摔在地上，粉身碎骨的。

第三步

CD-80

口才練功房：重新過招，學學「瑟夫里諾」的口氣、語調

Billy was nuts. Once he walked out / to the end of a beam / on the 38th floor. He stood at attention / facing out at the sky / and put'is hands together / lik'e was praying. Then he turned around, waved goodbye, and stepped off. We ran over / expecting to see'im splattered all over the ground. But he was hanging by one hand / from the underside of the beam, laughing. When he saw our scared faces, he laughed so hard he almost lost'is grip / and slipped off.

換你朗讀。特別注意：
1. 基本原則請參考 [序2]
2. 如果需要多聽幾次示範，請到 CD-80 [00:06]
3. 請注意停頓、語氣的表現：
　[/]：除了一般英文標點符號以外，可以停頓的地方。
　[套色字]：加重語氣的字。

第四步

如果需要再聽幾次，請重播 **CD-80** [00:06]

心法修練：重播 CD，測驗自己習得幾成功力

Billy was nuts. Once he walked out to the end of a beam on the 38th floor. He _____ facing out at the sky and _____ _____. Then he turned around, _____, and _____. We _____ expecting to see him _____ all over the ground. But he was _____ from the underside of the beam, laughing. When he saw our scared faces, he laughed so hard he almost _____ and _____.

第五步

變化招式：領悟基本動作的另一層意義

hang out 閒蕩；廝混

After working at the docks, Hatchet Hands liked to hang out with his friends. 在碼頭的工作結束後，快斧手喜歡和朋友廝混。

have a hang-up (about something) （某事引發的）焦慮感

He was in a car accident on Christmas Eve a few years ago, so he has a hang-up about the holiday season. That's why he didn't come to our Christmas party. 幾年前他在聖誕節前夕出過車禍，因此，每逢聖誕假日他都會有焦慮感。這是什麼他沒來參加我們聖誕節派對的原因。

get hung up on something 因某事而耽擱

I'm sorry I haven't finished with the drawings yet. I got hung up on some minor details. 很抱歉那些畫我還沒畫完。因為我得處理一些小細節，所以耽擱了。

[28]

SWAMP SWIMMING
沼澤之泳
Bird Watching 賞鳥

　　剛開始的時候，劉先生對我出國的事很不高興。他覺得我們應該每六個星期就拍一部片子，他還威脅說如果我不乖乖配合，就把我撤換掉。但《你死定了、你完蛋了》大賣座，之後劉先生就開始有不同的想法。他說我搞失蹤記，可能反而對宣傳有利。有一年，他甚至跟我一起出國。因為他有賞鳥的嗜好，我跟他說我知道一個很棒的賞鳥地點。

　　At first, Mr. Lau was upset about my trips. He thought we should be making a movie every six weeks and he threatened to replace me if I didn't cooperate. But *You're Dead, You're Done* was huge. After that, Mr. Lau started to see things differently. He said my disappearing act might actually be good for publicity. One year he even joined me on a trip. He'd taken up bird watching as a hobby. I told him I knew a good place for birds.

來看VCR：[德利卡‧艾伯史塔克，鳥類學家兼導遊，巴西南部潘塔納沼澤區]

One morning we're watching a giant Jabiru stork[1]. The old guy, Mr. Lau, gets so excited he <u>fumbles</u> a big telephoto lens out of the boat. <u>Plunk</u> — right into the swamp. The other guy <u>hops up</u>, starts to <u>peel off his shirt</u>. I say, "Bad idea. Leeches[2]. Piranha[3]. Caiman[4] — they're like alligators[5]." He <u>grins</u>, says he'll bring one back for me, and <u>dives in</u>. Two minutes later, he <u>splashes</u> up <u>spluttering</u>, laughing, <u>gasping for air</u>, holding the lens in one hand and a four-foot caiman by the snout in the other.

翻譯

　　一天早上，我們在觀看一隻大型裸頸鸛。那個老傢伙，劉先生，興奮過度，他笨手笨腳地把一個巨大的遠距鏡頭給掉出船外。噗通一聲──鏡頭就這麼掉進了沼澤中。另一個傢伙立刻跳出來，開始扒掉他的襯衫。我說：「不妥。水裡有水蛭、食人魚、還有凱門鱷──牠們就像短吻鱷。」他咧嘴微笑，說他會抓一隻上來給我，說著就跳進水裡。兩分鐘之後，他嘩啦一聲，嘴裡一面吐著水，一面大笑，還大口喘著氣。只見他一手拿著鏡頭，另一隻手抓住一隻四尺長凱門鱷的口鼻部。

Word list
1. Jabiru stork [`ˈjæbəruˈstɔrk] （熱帶美洲）長頸鸛
2. leech [litʃ] n. 水蛭
3. piranha [pɪˈranjə] n. 食人魚
4. caiman [`kemən] n. （中南美洲）凱門鱷
5. alligator [`æləˌgetə] n. 短吻鱷

177

第一步

動作分解：跟唸3-5次紮實基本功

o to fumble	笨拙處理
o to plunk	碰的一聲放下
o to hop up	跳出來
o to peel off [one's shirt]	扒掉（襯衫）
o to grin	露齒微笑
o to dive in	縱身跳入
o to splash	濺起水花
o to splutter	把口中的水吐出來
o to gasp for air	大口喘氣

第二步

發音秘笈：跟唸2-3次，破除你咬字含糊、發音錯誤的弱點

發音：長音 [i] vs. 短音 [ɪ]

很多人會把長音 [i] 和短音 [ɪ] 這兩個音搞混。請聽並比較以下兩組短字。注意，每組字的子音部分完全一樣，但母音卻不同。

[練習]

長音 [i]： eat | bean | greed | leap
短音 [ɪ]： it | bin | grid | lip

現在請試著唸出德利卡獨白中的一些字詞：

長音 [i]： peel | leech | he | me
短音 [ɪ]： big | into | grin | minute

He **grins**, says he'll **bring** one back for **me**.

第三步

CD-83

口才練功房：重新過招，學學「艾佰史塔克」的口氣、語調

One morning we're watching a giant Jabiru stork. The old guy, Mr. Lau, gets so excited / he fumbles a big telephoto lens out of the boat. Plunk — right into the swamp. The other guy hops up, starts to peel off his shirt. I say, "Bad idea. Leeches. Piranha. Caiman — they're like alligators." He grins, says he'll bring one back for me, and dives in. Two minutes later, he splashes up / spluttering, laughing, gasping for air, holding the lens in one hand / and a four-foot caiman by the snout in the other.

換你朗讀。特別注意：

1. 基本原則請參考 [序2]

2. 如果需要多聽幾次示範，請到 CD-83 [00:06]

3. 請注意停頓、語氣的表現：

  [/]：除了一般英文標點符號以外，可以停頓的地方。

  [套色字]：加重語氣的字。

如果需要再聽幾次，請重播CD-83 [00:06]

第四步

心法修練：重播CD，測驗自己習得幾成功力

One morning we're watching a giant Jabiru stork. The old guy, Mr. Lau, gets so excited he _____ a big telephoto lens out of the boat. _____ — right into the swamp. The other guy _____, starts to _____. I say, "Bad idea. Leeches. Piranha. Caiman — they're like alligators." He _____, says he'll bring one back for me, and _____. Two minutes later, he _____ up _____, laughing, _____, holding the lens in one hand and a four-foot caiman by the snout in the other.

第五步

變化招式：領悟基本動作的另一層意義

make a splash 引人注目

　　Joan made a splash at her new job by finding ten new corporate customers in her first week. 瓊安在新工作中的表現引人注目；她在第一個禮拜就找到了十個新的企業客戶。

a splash of color 增添些許色彩

　　The setting sun added a splash of color to the cloudy, gray sky. 落日為陰霾的天空增添了些許色彩。

a splash page 醒目的轉介首頁

　　Your home page is a little boring — why don't you add a splash page to spice it up a little? 你的首頁有一點無趣——何不加一個醒目的轉介首頁，增加一點趣味呢。

NOTE.

國家圖書館出版品預行編目資料

朗讀學英文：拳打腳踢這麼說 / Jeff Hammons
作；金振寧譯. -- 初版. -- 臺北市：貝塔，2005〔民
94〕
　　面；　　　公分
　　ISBN 957-729-537-1 （平裝）
　　1.英國語言- 學習方法 2. 朗誦

805.1　　　　　　　　　　　　　　94014894

朗讀學英文：拳打腳踢這麼說
Talk Like a Star — Action!

作　　者 / Jeff Hammons
審　　定 / 王復國
譯　　者 / 金振寧
執行編輯 / 陳玉娥

出　　版 / 貝塔語言出版有限公司
地　　址 / 台北市 100 館前路 12 號 11 樓
電　　話 / (02)2314-2525
傳　　真 / (02)2312-3535
郵　　撥 / 19493777 貝塔出版有限公司
客服專線 / (02)2314-3535
客服信箱 / btservice@betamedia.com.tw

總 經 銷 / 時報文化出版企業股份有限公司
地　　址 / 桃園縣龜山鄉萬壽路二段 351 號
電　　話 / (02) 2306-6842

出版日期 / 2005 年 9 月初版
定　　價 / 250 元
Ｉ Ｓ Ｂ Ｎ： 957-729-537-1

Talk Like a Star —Action! by Jeff Hammons
Copyright 2005 by Beta Multimedia Publishing
Published by Beta Multimedia Publishing

貝塔網址： www.betamedia.com.tw

喚醒你的英文語感 !

對折後釘好，直接寄回即可！

| 廣　告　回　信 |
| 北區郵政管理局登記證 |
| 北 台 字 第 1 4 2 5 6 號 |
| 免　貼　郵　票 |

100 台北市中正區館前路12號11樓

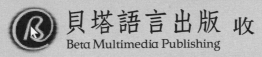

貝塔語言出版 收
Beta Multimedia Publishing

寄件者住址 □□□

貝塔語言出版
Beta Multimedia Publishing

讀者服務專線（02）2314-3535　　讀者服務傳真（02）2312-353□

客戶服務信箱　btservice@betamedia.com.tw

www.betamedia.com.tw

謝謝您購買本書！！

貝塔語言擁有最優良之英文學習書籍，為提供您最佳的英語學習資訊，您可填妥此表後寄回（免貼郵票）將可不定期收到本公司最新發行書訊及活動訊息！

姓名：_____　性別：□男 □女　生日：____年____月____日

電話：(公)_____(宅)_____(手機)_____

電子信箱：_____

學歷：□高中職含以下　□專科　□大學　□研究所含以上

職業：□金融　□服務　□傳播　□製造　□資訊　□軍公教　□出版

　　　□自由　□教育　□學生　□其他

職級：□企業負責人　□高階主管　□中階主管　□職員　□專業人士

1. 您購買的書籍是？_____

2. 您從何處得知本產品？(可複選)

　　　□書店 □網路 □書展 □校園活動 □廣告信函 □他人推薦 □新聞報導 □其他

3. 您覺得本產品價格：

　　　□偏高 □合理 □偏低

4. 請問目前您每週花了多少時間學英語？

　　　□ 不到十分鐘 □ 十分鐘以上，但不到半小時 □ 半小時以上，但不到一小時

　　　□ 一小時以上，但不到兩小時 □ 兩個小時以上 □ 不一定

5. 通常在選擇語言學習書時，哪些因素是您會考慮的？

　　　□ 封面 □ 內容、實用性 □ 品牌 □ 媒體、朋友推薦 □ 價格□ 其他_____

6. 市面上您最需要的語言書種類為？

　　　□ 聽力 □ 閱讀 □ 文法 □ 口說 □ 寫作 □ 其他_____

7. 通常您會透過何種方式選購語言學習書籍？

　　　□ 書店門市 □ 網路書店 □ 郵購 □ 直接找出版社 □ 學校或公司團購

　　　□ 其他_____

8. 給我們的建議：_____

_____

喚醒你的英文語感！

Get a Feel for English !

Get a Feel for English !

喚醒你的英文語感！